EXIT STRATEGY

EXIT STRATEGY

Lauren Allbright

ALADDIN

NEW YORK   LONDON   TORONTO   SYDNEY   NEW DELHI

This book is a work of fiction. Any references to historical events, real people, or real places are used fictitiously. Other names, characters, places, and events are products of the author's imagination, and any resemblance to actual events or places or persons, living or dead, is entirely coincidental.

ALADDIN

An imprint of Simon & Schuster Children's Publishing Division
1230 Avenue of the Americas, New York, New York 10020
First Aladdin hardcover edition June 2017
Text copyright © 2017 by Lauren Zutavern
Jacket design and illustration by Regina Flath, copyright © 2017 by Simon & Schuster, Inc.
Interior illustrations copyright © 2017 by Lauren Zutavern
All rights reserved, including the right of reproduction in whole or in part in any form.
ALADDIN and related logo are registered trademarks of Simon & Schuster, Inc.
For information about special discounts for bulk purchases, please contact
Simon & Schuster Special Sales at 1-866-506-1949 or business@simonandschuster.com.
The Simon & Schuster Speakers Bureau can bring authors to your live event.
For more information or to book an event contact the Simon & Schuster
Speakers Bureau at 1-866-248-3049 or visit our website at www.simonspeakers.com.
Interior designed by Nina Simoneaux
The illustrations for this book were rendered digitally.
The text of this book was set in Goudy Old Style.
Manufactured in the United States of America 0517 FFG
10 9 8 7 6 5 4 3 2 1
This book has been cataloged with the Library of Congress.
ISBN 978-1-4814-7912-7 (hc)
ISBN 978-1-4814-7914-1 (eBook)

To Zach.
And to Colton, Logan,
and Rowyn.

CONTENTS

FIGURES

TABLES

STATE THE PROBLEM
OR QUESTION

What are you trying to find out?

From: nomadman@nma.com

To: herecomeztreble@nma.com

Subject: A Swimming Success

So, all went as planned—actually better. Was totally Fish-tastic. I'll tell you more when I'm on the computer instead of Mom's phone, but the record holds. Would have been suspended if I hadn't already been leaving, they said.

And guess what? Mom said yes! She's going to call your mom and work it out, but she said she thinks I can stay with you for the entire week. Ahh!

Now to wait the million days until summer is here. Can't wait to see your house and meet all your friends. You'll have to make them wear name tags or something so I can keep up.

On our way to St. Louis. Three months there. Already got Exit-lence plans in the works. Will be epic. Stinks you aren't around to see it. Though I guess my fame wouldn't be imminent if you and your mom hadn't bailed. I'm only, like, 23% mad at you (or at least your mom) now.

Ross

PEOPLE CAN SPEND their entire lives trying to achieve greatness, but I am fortunate—at the age of twelve, I already know it.

It was by dumb luck that I'd found my "great" to begin with. Before The Incident at the end of fifth grade, I was just a kid that moved a lot.

For moves One through Seven, my school exits consisted of all the normal stuff: shove my eraser-less pencils and half-used spirals into my backpack, mosey up to the front of the classroom, and wave good-bye to kids I barely knew. They'd collectively say "bye" and wave back. After a hug from a teacher who wouldn't remember me past recess, I'd be on my unmerry way to my next school.

Move Eight, however, was when the happy accident happened. With all of my school-ly possessions in my bag, I started my moderately paced shuffle toward the door—slow enough that I looked appropriately sad and eager enough that I didn't look depressed. Unfortunately, I didn't see Shana Miller's messenger bag strap until *after* it was wrapped around my foot like a booby trap. When it snagged me, I tried to stay upright, flinging my arms out and attempting to win my fight with gravity by grabbing the desks on either side of me. But my last day there also happened to be one of those days the teacher felt the need to rid herself of all of old worksheets, and both of the desks I grabbed were covered with stacks of papers (see Figure 1). My hands slid out from me and down

    down

    down

    I went.

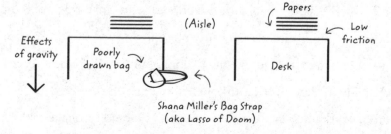

Figure 1. Effects of gravity on a falling body

My left elbow and right knee took most of the fall. My lips pressed together to hold back my yell. Tears sprang to my eyes. All of that old work fluttered down beside me like the ashes of my pride.

And then: dead silence.

Nobody knew what to do. Should they laugh? Help? Pretend it didn't happen?

Me, on the other hand, I knew I had two options:

I could stand up and bawl as they sent me off in a chorus of good-byes and forever live in their memories as a fifth grade baby.

OR

Get up, say bye, and get the heck out of there before the dam broke.

Opting for the second, I carefully removed the strap from my ankle and scrambled to my feet. I grabbed my bag off the floor and dared to peek at my audience before offering my best wishes.

But I froze.

Every. Single. Eye was on me. Even the kid in the back with the thick glasses and multi-directional stare managed to train both his pupils directly upon my presence. My chin and bottom lip shook like the suspicious-looking Jell-O salad they served that day in the cafeteria. If I opened my mouth or waved or even *breathed*, the floodgates would open and I would look like a blubbering idiot. A baby. A blubbering-idiot-baby.

Nope. Words were *not* an option.

So, in a gust of brilliance, I abandoned my verbal skills, threw both of my hands up like a V for victory, bowed, and ran out of the classroom.

Before the door closed, I heard the laughing.

For one second, I thought they were laughing *at* me, but before I was out of earshot I heard one kid say, "That was *awesome!*" and I knew they were laughing *because* of me. It was a victory. One I planned to enjoy after I attended to my blubbering-idiot-baby-ness in private.

I remember pushing through that swinging door of the boys' bathroom, ready to let out the tears I'd assumed had built up after my fall. I sat in the last stall—the big one—and squeezed my eyes shut and waited, but nothing came.

Not quite believing my fast beating heart was caused by adrenaline rather than the threat of crying, I waited some more. Still nothing.

I tried squeezing at the tear ducts the way I saw my mom do if she got a pimple.

But still, I was dry as a desert.

That was when, to my shock and exhilaration, I realized I didn't feel bad at all. Instead, I felt . . . heroic. Memorable. Funny.

And it changed my *life*.

* · * · *

MY EXITS FOLLOWING that day were marvelous. Stellar. Epic. EXIT-LENT. And not by accident. I planned my exits from the moment I knew I was transferring to a new school until the day I left. Each escape was better than the last (see Figure 2, and note: From the following data you will see that I over-thought Move Nine but recovered by Move Ten).

I flat out *owned* today's finale: Move Eleven.

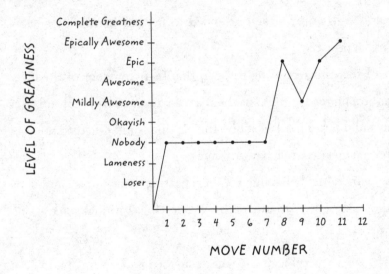

Figure 2. Measure of greatness for each move

Though I gladly pay it, my victories do come at a price. The drive to mom's next tour stop—our next home—always gives her plenty of time for the standard post-Exit-lence lecture, and today is no exception. This is most painful part of the process; I've learned to brave these post-Exit-lence lectures and even shorten them by arranging my face into an expression that is equal parts sad and apologetic.

Today I do not catch a break. The lecture is twenty-three minutes long. It starts with phrases like *respect for authority* and *common decency*. It ends with *failure as a mother* and *unreasonable expectations for both of us*.

"You are such a good kid," she says as she's winding down. "It's like you're just missing it. Like you don't get when you're crossing the line. You don't even give people a chance to like you."

After she ends with the standard, "I just don't know how to know if I'm doing the right thing," we are both quiet for a good four minutes. Then, like normal, my mom takes a deep breath and pats my knee. The stressful part is over. We can move on to the pep rally part where she tells me that she knows it is hard to move *again*, and she knows I miss my best friend, Trent, and she knows it's different since he and his mom stopped touring with the symphony.

Approximately seven minutes after her closing statement, I pull out my notebook and begin to think about my next exit strategy, my future finale, aka Move Twelve. The planning is exciting—but I'm careful not to let it show on my face. I need to look thoughtful for at least twelve more minutes, or I'll have to sit through Lecture, Part Two.

It's hard to look guilty though, because I've already got a few really great ideas. My next finale will be spectacular. Like Complete Greatness level. Fireworks will be involved. My next Exit-lence could be famous-making. Kids will ask for my autograph, teachers will praise my creativity, there will be Facebook fan clubs devoted to me. Basically, for Move Twelve, I will be epic (see Table 1).

Table 1. Achievement of Exit-lence

MOVE	PLAN NAME	MATERIALS NEEDED	PROCEDURE	CONCLUSION
1	Moving Day	Mom gets another job	Walk of lame to the front. Say goodbye	Blah and bleck.
2	Here We Go Again	"	"	"
3	Losers-R-Us	"	"	"
4	Same-O Lame-O	"	"	"
5	Incredible Forgettable	"	"	"
6	Super Power: Invisibility	"	"	"
7	Here Today, Gone Tomorrow	"	"	"
8	Dumb Luck (See Figure 1)	Excess papers passed back. Sloppy students leaving their bags in the aisle. Genetic clumsiness and lack of coordination.	Get my foot caught on Shana's bag and fall in front of everybody. Played it off like I meant to be an idiot.	Life changing experience.

continued on next page →

9	Just Dumb	No papers. Fake forced fall. Tried to recreate previous exit.	Tried too hard. But class was so bored, they laughed anyway.	Lesson learned. Go big or go home.
10	Cry Me a River	Salt. Lots of salt. Teachers that need coffee like they need air.	Early arrival to "pack my stuff." Undercaffeinated teachers that didn't pay attention to the kid in the teachers' lounge.	Discovery of weak gag reflexes among teachers. The beginning of my infamy. (Near-Suspension #1)
11	Something's Fishy	Twenty-six goldfish. Pretend trip to the bathroom to allegedly compose myself.	One goldfish per toilet.	Better than I could have hoped for. Kids were peeing outside until the janitor scooped fish out. (Near-Suspension #2)
12	Super Power: Awesomeness Embodied	Sparklers. No way to enforce consequences.	Still in the works.	The stuff legends are made of.

I pause in my plans and borrow Mom's phone to send an e-mail to my best friend, Trent. Right after I press send, the phone rings. It's a number I don't recognize, so I hand it back to Mom.

"Hello," she says. And then, "Yes, it is."

Her wide, panicked eyes make me freeze. There are only three things in the world Mom cares about enough to make her freak out—and two of them are in this car.

"Thank you for calling," Mom says. She puts on her blinker and changes lanes. "We're coming right now. Please call if anything changes." She drops the phone and exits the highway.

"What's wrong?" I ask. Her sharp U-turn makes the phone slide over the console and fall on the floorboard.

"It's Pops," she says naming the third thing.

SINCE MOM AND I move every couple of months (give or take), we don't keep a lot of stuff. Everything we own—including her three bassoons—fits inside our Suburban. This means it is super easy to relocate. It also means that when we get a phone call that mom's dad (my Pops) fell and went to the hospital, unconscious, in an ambulance, we can change our plans midroute and break the speed limit to get to him.

Mom's so quiet as she drives. Both hands squeeze the steering wheel and she leans forward like it will make us get to Pops even faster. I want to tell her it'll be okay, but since I don't really know if that's true, I don't.

When the phone rings again, she snatches it up. Her hands are shaking as she taps the screen to answer. She says "hello" and then nods even though the person on the other end can't see her.

"Oh, thank you," she says. "Thank you so much. Please tell him we're coming. We'll be there in a little under an hour. Tell him to rest . . . and we love him."

She puts the phone on the seat and I glance at it to make sure it's hung up.

"He's awake," Mom tells me and she smiles. She turns on the radio. I didn't even realize we'd been driving in complete silence.

When we pull into the hospital parking lot, we've been in the car for seven hours straight. Still, we don't take time to stretch before we go inside to find Pops.

He's awake when we come into his room. His eyes are open and watery, and he's staring at the ceiling. When Mom says, "Hi, Daddy," he turns toward us and smiles. The liquid in his right eye slips out and falls as a tear down his face, slowing on his deepest wrinkles. It's only been about three months since we saw him last, but from the way he's changed, it seems like it should be years.

He holds a hand out to us and Mom grabs it. He smiles bigger and nods. Then his head tilts to the side and he falls asleep. Seriously, it's that fast. One second he's awake and the next second he isn't.

I glance at Mom to make sure we didn't just see him, like, die or something. She's studying the computer screen to the side of the bed and not panicking at all, so I'm guessing it's okay.

Mom sits in a chair next to Pops so she doesn't have to let go of his hand while he sleeps, and I sit in the chair next to the window. She says I can watch TV, but it would feel weird to channel surf while Pops is lying there, so I tell her I'm okay and take out my Exit-lence notebook to plan. But it's like all the machines in here are blocking my brainwaves and I can't think of anything to add.

The doctor comes in a little bit later to talk to us. He looks like every other doctor I've ever seen, except he's wearing cowboy boots with his scrubs. He shakes Mom's free hand and then mine, and tells us stuff we already know from the calls—Pops fell; he's got a tiny brain bleed; he's not himself. Then he tells us that he believes with the right help, Pops will be okay. After a couple of days at the hospital, he'll go to a different place to get physical therapy. Dr. Cowboy Boots says he's feeling hopeful Pops will make a full recovery . . . eventually.

"Oh, thank you," Mom practically yells. It's like she wants to hug the doctor but she doesn't want to let go of her dad and she makes up for it with an extra-loud voice. It wakes Pops up. We watch him as his eyes get big and confused and he searches the room until he focuses on his hand and follows the chain of arms to Mom and then me. He smiles again—this time bigger than a kid that got a pony for Christmas.

"It's going to be okay," Mom says to him. Then she looks at me. "It's going to be okay." And because she's my mom, I believe her.

MOM SITS AT Pops's kitchen table and calls the director of the touring company. She tells him we've had a family emergency and we aren't going to make it to St. Louis. Before she hangs up, she says he may want to hire a local musician for the stop after St. Louis too.

We're staying at Pops's house even though he isn't. Last night we unloaded the car and tried to settle in. We put all my boxes in the room with the twin bed and all of Mom's in the office with the pullout couch. I told her she should take the bed and I could take the couch because I'm younger. She mommed me and said I needed more sleep because I'm still growing (and since I'm shorter than average, I couldn't argue).

Most of this feels normal for us. As we tour, we rent houses or apartments that already have all the practical stuff: furniture, dishes, pots and pans. All we bring is our clothes and anything we think is worth packing up and hauling around—like Mom's awards or my football cards—even if we don't ever actually unbox it. We both know the routine, so I'm not surprised when Mom tells me it's time to go up to the school to get me registered.

We go up to the school in the middle of the day. The lady at the front desk checks our papers and send us to the counselor, Mrs. Jackson. Her office is big. She sits behind a desk and we sit in the armchairs facing her. There's no windows. There's tons of lamps though. It feels like a well-lit dungeon.

After Mom hands her the folder of my school records, Mrs. Jackson has the standard reaction: surprise followed by intense interest and careful reading. Mom and I are quiet as she looks at every school transcript. She must be an extra thorough counselor, because she starts again from the beginning.

"Yes, it *is* a lot of schools," Mom interrupts the second reading by answering the question we know is coming. "My job keeps us moving."

The counselor looks up and closes the folder on her lap. "Your job?"

"A bassoonist with the St. Louis Touring Company. Like for actors? But I'm in the orchestra. I play in one location for a couple months or so and then move to the next location."

Mrs. Jackson nods. "Sometimes we find children that have attended a succession of schools were . . ." She looks at the ceiling like the word she wants is written up there. I glance up to see if it is, but there are just shadows. ". . . were getting into trouble," she says. "They withdraw from their previous school before the bad behavior goes on their permanent record."

"That's not Ross. We just move because of my job."

The counselor nods and glances through my records again. Mom takes the opportunity to give me a side-eye warning and a tiny head shake. I think she's worried I'll correct her and confess my near-suspensions. I never would do that though—it's much easier for me to get away with the Exit-lence when nobody's expecting me to do it.

Mom sits up straighter and scoots to the edge of her chair. Her hands twitch like she wants to snatch the folder away.

"He used to have a tutor," Mom blurts, going off-script. "Until he was in third grade he had a tutor—it was like homeschool sort of. Just not at a home."

Mrs. Jackson nods and flips to another paper.

"Two of us had kids, my friend and me—I had Ross and she had Trent. The tutor traveled with us and taught our boys. But my friend won a permanent position. She stopped touring—and a tutor didn't make sense for just one kid. I mean he's worth it, but it was really expensive. And I thought he should have some normal school experience, you know? Like with social stuff and all that." Mom forces a laugh. "That's an important part of school, right?"

The counselor doesn't answer.

Mom rolls her shoulders back like she's trying to relax; she smooths her shirt down and clears her throat.

My leg starts shaking; Mom's nervousness is contagious. And confusing. She performs in front of thousands of people six times a week and this is the first time I've ever seen her like this.

"So Ross does public school." She looks at me and smiles. I smile back. "But we still move. He's been to a lot of schools. It's because of my job. Not because he gets into trouble." She nods at me like I'm supposed to say something. "Right, Ross?"

"Um. Yes. Her job." The trouble only comes as we leave.

"Well," Mrs. Jackson says as she turns in her chair and gets a paper out of her desk drawer. She swivels back around. "I hope you'll be able to stay a while here. We feel like our school is a pretty great place to be."

"You sound like my father!" Mom says, then adds, "Your words, not your voice. His is much deeper. And he can't talk right now."

Both my legs are wiggling now. And my right hand.

Mom blinks hard like she's trying to reset. "Yes. You're right. We're glad to be here."

Which happens to be the exact opposite of what I'm currently thinking. Even after Mom fills out all the paperwork, I get my schedule (see Table 2), and we take a tour of the school. Even before I get Trent's reply, I have a bad feeling about this.

Table 2. Student Schedule: Ross Stevens

MONDAY	TUESDAY	WEDNESDAY	THURSDAY	FRIDAY
Math Mr. Longfellow	Math Mr. Longfellow	Math Mr. Longfellow	Math Mr. Longfellow	Math Mr. Longfellow
Specials: P.E.*	Specials: Art	Specials: Music	Specials: P.E.*	Specials: Spanish
Science Ms. Harding	Science Ms. Harding	Science Ms. Harding	Science Ms. Harding	Science Ms. Harding
Lunch	Lunch	Lunch	Lunch	Lunch
Recess	Recess	Recess	Recess	Recess
Language Arts Ms. Wahl	Language Arts Ms. Wahl	Language Arts Ms. Wahl	Language Arts Ms. Wahl	Language Arts Ms. Wahl
Social Studies Ms. Noel	Social Studies Ms. Noel	Social Studies Ms. Noel	Social Studies Ms. Noel	Social Studies Ms. Noel

*Please wear tennis shoes on days you have P.E.

From: nomadman@nma.com

To: herecomeztreble@nma.com

Subject: Change of Plans

No St. Louis after all.

My grandfather fell and hit his noggin. We got
a call and came straight there. Was kinda freaky
for a while because for, like, two hours we didn't
know if he'd be okay. (He will be, but it'll take
a while.) Everything was already loaded in our
car for the move, so we just drove to Fort Worth
instead. Isn't that a little closer to San Antonio?

It's my first time visiting anybody in a hospital. It
stinks—the actual smell of it, I mean.

By the time we got here, he was awake. He
still hasn't talked yet though. He's got a bruise
across both eyes and down one side of his
cheek. Don't think it looks as bad as the one
I got when I fell out of that harness they used
in Peter Pan when we didn't get the strap on
right.

I've told Pops about a bunch of the stuff we've done. Mom told me to talk to him even if he can't talk back. He can't laugh yet, but he smiled really big and did these two deep breath things that made me think he was cracking up inside.

So, anyway, here I am in Fort Worth. Starting school tomorrow. Moving day is TBD until Pops gets better and then we'll be off again.

Ross

— — — — — — — — — — — — — — —

From: herecomeztreble@nma.com
To: nomadman@nma.com
Subject: Re: Change of Plans

You're staying put? (At least for now?) This a pretty big deal for you. Like, gigantic.

And I know you already know it's not like when Mr. Bob tutored us, but it's also nothing like the school stops you are used to. It's been three years for me and I'm just now not considered the new kid. And that's me—you know I'm pretty cool with anything. Mom always says I can talk to a wall.

As your best friend and somebody that has known you forever, I'm going to help you out. You know how Mr. Bob used to say stuff like, *Everybody has something to offer* and, *Always ask questions* and, *Stay curious*? DO NOT listen to that. It's old man advice. Only one of his sayings actually applies to the real and modern world, and it is, *Be yourself, but better.* When you walk in there tomorrow, be SOMEBODY. Like, be you, but better. Find the varsity team and stick with them.

Gotta go to baseball. More later.

T

As Mom is driving me to my first day at my new school, I tell myself I can do this. The school-with-no-end-date thing. Especially with Trent's advice.

I've totally got this. Mostly. Probably. Sort of.

If Trent can do it, so can I. I mean, between the two of us, I was the one with the endless ideas. I was the one that could turn a boring afternoon into a something amazing. My plans only sent us to the ER twice. Trent just went along with whatever I came up with. That's my strength. That's how I can do what Trent said: Be myself, but better.

"Just drop me off in front," I tell Mom. No need for me to be the only kid that still has his mom walk him inside.

I only feel a little like throwing up when I get out of the car.

I can do this.

I take a deep breath and start walking, one foot in front of the other.

"Got your bag?" Mom calls out through the open passenger-side window.

I don't. I never remember details when I'm super nervous. I go back to the car and grab my backpack. I really want to climb back inside. The car is safe.

"So you'll take the bus home after school," she reminds me. Her smile is so forced, she looks like the Joker from Batman. I can tell she doesn't feel good about this either.

"You know, I'm thinking I should just go ahead and leave with you right now."

She frowns. "Ross," she says, "please . . ." She bites her lips together.

I am the worst. Her dad is in the hospital. She had to bow out of her gig. And now I'm going to make her worry about me, too. "I'm kidding."

She bites her lip and nods. "Okay."

Mom stays parked as I walk up the steps to the school and pull open the first set of double doors. I wave to show her I'm fine and step inside. I take a deep breath before pushing through the second set of doors.

Here I go. A new school. But I'm used to this, right? Who cares if I don't know how long I'll actually be here?

Be better, Ross.

The bell hasn't rung yet and kids are lined up on either side of the hallway when I walk in. If there was music playing somewhere in the distance, it would screech and go silent.

Conversations stop. Kids gawk. As if they are sharing one brain, everybody turns to look at me. I force myself to move forward even though my legs feel heavy and my mouth is soooo dry.

This reminds me of something I saw one time when I was little and I used to sneak out of my room at night to get water and watch TV—neither of which was allowed after bedtime. One night, after I rehydrated myself from the bathroom sink, I crept into the living room and turned on the television, immediately muting it so I didn't get caught. I couldn't hear anything, but I didn't need the words. I watched as a policeman led a dude in an orange jumpsuit down a prison hallway toward an electric chair.

Like greedy zombies, hands reached out from the cells on either side of him. Then he sat in a wired-up chair and got burned like my mom's cooking. Back then it freaked me out so bad that I ran back to my room and turned on all the lights. When I finally fell asleep, I dreamed I was the guy being led to my doom and the people were trying to touch *me*. (I also dreamed of a toilet at the end of that long hallway, but I won't go into that.)

Now, as my shoes squeak on the shiny floor, again I am the prisoner walking down the wide fluorescent-lit hallway. Except instead of convicts, it is lined with my newest classmates, instead of hands they reach for me with their stares, and instead of an electric chair, there is an office—but still, it's certain death. And it's not a dream.

This is wrong. This isn't how I normally feel. Starting a new school is great; it's exciting. I'm the new kid—I don't have to make friends or do projects because we'll be leaving in a few months or so. School is an event. A performance. Except this time it isn't.

Be better, Trent had said. Focus on that. A better me. But what does that even mean? I am nothing here. How can I be a better nothing?

I cannot keep walking. I freeze.

I cannot breathe.

My chest is spastic, beating with the enthusiasm of a thousand hard-of-hearing drummers.

I am having a heart attack.

Can seventh graders even have heart attacks?

If it hasn't happened before, it's happening now.

I need help. I need somebody to call an ambulance.

To call my mom.

To give me CPR. (Gross!)

But there's nobody I know, nobody I can ask.

I cannot take another step forward.

Why have my lungs stopped working? And why did they turn the heat in this school up to one million degrees?

Nope, my brain says. And my body agrees.

Nope. Nope. Nope.

Energy floods my elbows and knees and tells me to run and I don't have any choice but to listen.

I spin around, back toward the doors.

I walk at first, then I speed up to a full run. Whispers explode around me. They are talking about me. Of course they are, because I'm totally freaking out.

I don't even care because I'm almost out of there.

I push through the double doors. I search for Mom's car, but it's gone.

So I do the only thing I can. I run.

And run.

I only slow down when the voice in my head that says I need

oxygen is louder than the one that tells me I need to get away.

Pops doesn't live far from the school. Surely I should be back at his house by now, but I recognize nothing. Or more accurately, I recognize *everything* because it is all generic. It's all the same. Every trash can. Every grass type. Every tree height. Why did my grandfather pick such a plastic place to live?

My breathing speeds up again as reality sets in: *I don't know where I am.*

And it keeps getting worse.

I don't have a phone to call my mom. I don't know how to get to Pops's house. I don't have a chance to recover from the humiliation that is currently seeping in like the damp wind through my jacket.

I'm out in the open. And lost.

I wind around the backs of the houses to an alley that could be Pops's or could be somebody else's. I sink down between two bushes with pointy leaves that catch my sleeves and scratch my arms.

Nobody will know to look for me here.

I can freak out in peace. I could hide here forever if I wanted.

And I do. Want to, I mean. And I probably can, because there is no one that knows me; they won't come find me; they won't even know to tell my mom I am missing.

* ° * ° *

I'M SITTING ON my borrowed bed leaning against the wooden headboard with my feet straight out on the comforter; I'm waiting for Mom to form a solid sentence. My shoes are still on, but she hasn't noticed and made me take them off. She sits at the end of the bed with her back straight as a ruler and her hands in her lap. I try to concentrate on anything but her—the framed picture on the dresser, the bare tree outside the window, the open closet with boxes of clothes that I dig through in the mornings to get dressed—but eventually I can't help but peek at her. She stares straight ahead, takes a deep breath, opens her mouth like she is going to speak, and then shuts it and sighs again. She repeats this cycle for a solid nine minutes.

Finally, I help her out. "You can yell at me if you want."

She brings her hands to her face, covers her eyes, and shakes her head. "I'm not going to yell at you."

"You might feel better."

"Oh, honey," she says and puts both of her hands on my left leg, then pulls one back to cover her mouth as if that is where her tears are about to leak out.

My nose burns a little and I scratch it to make it stop.

"I love you," she says.

I don't know what to say to make this better. She has probably been thinking about punishments from the moment the school called to tell her I was absent to the moment she found me wandering around the neighborhood with streets so circular I was like a brainless mouse in a maze.

So I say, "I need it," using our code. An *I love you* back means *I'm fine*. An *I need it* means *I will be fine, but not quite yet*. We've perfected this complex secret language over the past few years.

"I love you," I add, so she knows I know I deserve whatever consequence she's about to give me.

My words break her trance. She squeezes my leg and lets go. "Just tell me why you ran away." She scoots farther onto the bed and turns toward me. My breath catches when I see the actual tears. I am the one that is supposed to make Mom happy, not the one that makes her cry.

"I don't know," I say, and my voice cracks. What I mean is, *I'm soooooooooooo sorry*, but I can't talk anymore at the moment.

"Did something happen after I dropped you off?"

I shake my head. "Nothing happened." That's the problem. The nothing. The endless nothing with no end date. The nothingness where I am a nobody. Days and days full of it. This is Trent's area of expertise. I am the one that keeps moving. I've got no skills, nothing in my wheelhouse for this.

I clear my throat and shrug. "I don't want to stay here. That's not what we do."

"It's only until Pops gets better—it's not for forever," she says.

"It feels like it might as well be."

"Do you not like this school?"

She is leaning in, waiting for my answer. I think about telling her that *is* the problem. But then I could end up serving this sentence at a worse place—like where the P.E. equipment predates Abraham Lincoln and the grumpy lunch lady has a moustache. At this school they have a rock wall in the gym and the gray-haired lunch lady seemed nice enough, even if, when I met her on the school tour, I found she does wear a pill-y old sweater and have a tiny bit of ear hair. If I *had* to choose any school indefinitely, this one's okay (see Figure 3).

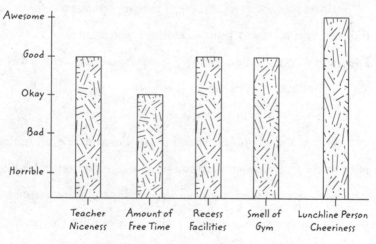

Figure 3. Assessment of current school

"It's fine," I say.

"So why did you run?"

I don't want to say what I am thinking out loud—that I don't know who I am if I'm not the temporary kid, the Exit-lence guy. That ZERO x BETTER = ZERO. Because it is embarrassing. Because she'll tell me again this isn't a forever thing, and she doesn't understand that not having a circled date on the calendar feels like forever to me. And because if I go down that path, she'll say she thinks she's failing as a mother. So I just shrug and say, "I don't know."

Mom wipes her eyes and blows her nose with a wadded-up tissue. She puts it in her lap and then grabs my wrist. Her hand is still a little damp. Yuck.

"Will you promise me," she says, "I mean, *promise* me that you will never, ever run away from school again? For three hours after the school called me I didn't know where you were. I just . . . three *hours* . . ." She starts crying again.

Guilt floods me. "I promise."

"Ross, you almost got suspended today. Before you even *started* your new school. Do you understand what a big deal that is? It's like you're trying to prove that counselor right. That you *are* a trouble-maker. Is that who you want to be?" She bites her lips together.

"Mom, I understand. I get it. I promise I won't do it again."

"I mean, *never*. Promise me. Promise me you'll follow the rules."

"Never," I say. "I promise I will go to school. I promise I won't get suspended." She relaxes like I've given her the correct answer.

"And," her voice softens, "you'll try to make it work. For now.

For me. So I can be here for Pops. You know, I know that as soon as the kids at your school get to know you, you'll be fighting them off with a stick. Can you just trust me until then? That is this is for the best?"

I nod. "Although I probably *will* get suspended if I'm hitting my friends with a stick."

She smiles, barely, and stands up. She smooths her hair back and pulls her shirt down to straighten up, but it doesn't help. She still looks sad. A sad I caused.

This is when she has super-mom-powers. When she can make me do anything, agree to anything if I know it will make her feel better. I force a smile and say, "I just freaked out earlier. So much is going on—the change of plans and Pops in the hospital. I'm better now; I'm glad we're here."

Her brave-face wavers. Her voice cracks when she adds, "I think I'm doing the right thing. With you. With Daddy. You think so, right? And we can be happy here for a little bit."

I sit up straighter. "I think so." I lie.

"Good. You do your homework. I'll let you know when dinner is ready, and then we'll go visit Pops."

After she's gone, I squeeze my hands into fists and try to put all the yuck inside them so I can force it out. I tell myself that it'll be okay. That I will like it here for however long we have to stay. That I don't have to be the kid with the exit strategy just yet.

But instead of my brain agreeing, it plays all my past school exits in my head like a highlight reel. Move One: I was Nobody. Move Two: I was Nobody. Move Three: I was Nobody. It keeps going. When I left, nobody cared. Nobody even noticed me until Move Eight. That's when I learned how to be awesome, how to be great, how to be funny. It's when I learned how to be somebody.

Is that even possible here?

My brain's as blank as the last time I tried to plan my Exitlence.

I need a distraction, so I open the absent-kid folder they sent home for me and pull out my assignments, thankful for something else to think about besides my expired greatness or today's Houdini act that my mom told the school was because of an upset stomach and a fear of public vomiting.

Math first. It's easy enough because no matter which school I go to, numbers are always the same. Then language arts. I have a little trouble doing my reading assignment, but only because I read a sentence then think about all the stuff I am trying not to think about and forget what I read. Eventually that is checked off my list too.

Then I pull out my last missed assignment. It's a packet of papers from science. The top says, "Elm Creek Middle School Science Fair Project."

I've seen assignments like this before, but I've never actually done one. I was always coming or going or new enough that the teachers didn't think I could handle it—and who was I to tell them otherwise?

I don't want to do it now.

I skim through the five pages—*five pages*—explaining the project. The major due date for this thing is, like, two months away, but there's a bunch dates where parts of it are due between now and then.

It makes me want to run away again.

I reread the first sheet.

The first due date is tomorrow. My homework tonight is to answer the first question.

I think about writing *The PROBLEM is that I don't understand the QUESTION*, but then I picture the counselor reading my paper and crossing her arms being all, like, I-told-you-so, and Mom's super-powered-sad-face, and I remember my promise to try.

I go to the computer and click on the Internet icon. When Google pops ups, I type in Science Project Questions and click on the first website. It has a list of potential science fair questions.

Do plants and animal behave differently with music?

Does food dye hurt plants?

Do video games reduce the ability to focus?

These all sound boring. I don't want to waste any time on

boring stuff because I'm just killing time. By the time the actual project is due, we'll probably already be settled at our next stop.

NAME _____

ELM CREEK MIDDLE SCHOOL
Science Fair Project

1. **State the problem or question.** What are you trying to find out?

2. **Develop a hypothesis.** Make a statement based on what you think the results will be.

3. **Research your problem.** Identify what you already know about this problem or question. What do you need to find out? What research needs to be done? (Minimum of 3 resources.)

4. **List the materials you will use.** What do you need to complete your investigation?

5. **Test your hypothesis.** Record and describe the observations you made during your investigation.

6. **Record the results/organize your data.** Include tables, charts, and graphs.

7. **Interpret the data and state your conclusion.** Was your hypothesis true? Was your big question answered?

8. **Additional research and information.** Include any other important observations and/or notes.

Figure 4. Science fair project assignment

How about: *When can we get out of here and move on with our lives?* But I can't use that—it only has one available resource and I've already made her cry today.

Maybe something more useful than that, like: *How do I make friends?*

Right. Because nothing says LOSER like a big trifold board about making friends.

What do I really want to know?

How can I be me, but better? How can I be fantastic without the finale? How can I once again be great?

I think about my Exit-lence, my exit strategies. Maybe I can break them down into parts and subtract the exit part (for now). Then when I add it back in, my finales will be fantastic-er.

Our tutor, Mr. Bob, told Trent and me that if you needed to take something away, you removed it from both sides to see what you had left, and that most things can be figured out with an equation. If you use the stuff you do know, you can figure out what you don't.

So, what do I know (see Figure 5)?

Exit-lence = Greatness	Exit-lence = Finale + Fantastic	Fantastic = Plan + Funny
So, Exit-lence = Finale + (Plan + Funny) Then subtract Finale from both sides, which equals		
Exit-lence − Finale = Plan + Funny	And if a = b and b = c, then a = c	
So, Greatness − Finale = Plan + Funny		
So, Greatness without Finale means I need a plan to be Funny.		

Figure 5. Formula explaining the necessity of funny

So the question asks: *What do I want to understand?* And the answer is: *If I need to understand how to be Me, But Better, I need to understand how to be funny.*

Which is still pretty lame.

Plus, who has to study to be funny? Not anybody that actually is.

That's okay though. I'll never actually present this. My project will be for my own personal research. Something to fill in the blanks for what the teacher's making me do. We'll be gone before I have to present it. And if I understand how to be funny, it'll make me better. I'll be fluent in funny. Like a second language, I'll speak Hilarious.

I've really got nothing to lose. So, in an act of bravery, I write the thing I need to make me better. Under *State the problem or question*, I write: *I'm going to discover how to be funny.*

DEVELOP A HYPOTHESIS

Make a statement based on what you think the results will be.

I'VE SUCCESSFULLY MADE it through two and a half classes without running away, when my science teacher, Ms. Harding, says, "Mr. Stevens, can you come here for a moment please?"

I stand up and arrange my pencil on top of my paper to cover my writing, but it doesn't hide enough. I flip the page over instead. I don't want anybody to see my brainstorming—because surprise is a HUGE part of being funny. And because I'll look super dumb if somebody reads it, which sort of works against my goal.

When I get to her desk, Ms. Harding removes her glasses from her face and lets them hang from the gold chain around her neck. She nods to a paper, *my* paper, that I turned in earlier and says, "Welcome again to our school." I tell her thank you and she says, "This is an . . . intriguing topic you've chosen here." Her words sound encouraging, but she's frowning so I know she didn't call me up to compliment my braininess.

"Okay," I say, waiting for the real reason.

For a moment she studies me, then she slides her glasses back on, picks up my paper, and silently reads my answer with her lips moving and no sound coming out. When she's done she leans back in her chair, crosses her arms, and takes her glasses off once again. "And how do you plan to test this?"

I relax a little. I know the answer to this from the packet I read. "With research and experimentation."

"Yes, yes, I know that." She shakes her hand like she's shooing away my answer. Her bracelets clink together. "But what *specifically*?"

"Specifically? Like, um, with controls. And variables."

"Yes, but *how* do you plan to research and experiment?"

"Oh, um . . ." I point to my desk. "I've been doing what you said to do. Brainstorming."

She clasps her hands together and rests them on my paper. The bracelets clink together. All one hundred of them. Probably one to represent every year she's taught. "Science tends to be . . . measurable. Able to be reproduced. What you're proposing is very . . . subjective. Don't you think?"

I'm still trying to understand her question when she tilts her head and answers it herself. "But there *are* the behavior sciences. They use surveys and the like." She tilts her head back to its first position. "Although surveys are so unreliable . . ." She sits up straight and turns to me. "Is the intent of this study on the purveyor or the receiver of the humor?"

"Ummmm," I say, and I hear a couple of kids giggle. When I glance at them, they laugh more.

Please, Floor, swallow me now.

I pretend to focus on my paper and reread my answer, even though her hands are still covering it.

"Thoughts, Mr. Stevens?" she says like she's been waiting for me to answer for hours.

"Well, um, my goal is to understand what is . . . ," I lean down and whisper, "funny. So I can . . . um, do it."

Her expression is stone. I can't tell if I'm hot or cold with my answer.

"Hmmm. Give me an example. How would you know if it was funny or not?" she says, resting her face on her palms. More clanking. More stares. More giggles.

"Well," I say, as quietly as I can, "laughter is a good measure. Like, for example, some people may laugh when they see somebody feeling really, *really* awkward when they're in front of the entire class. Talking to the teacher. About his science fair project. When he just really wants to sit down so people will stop looking at him."

"Okay," she says too loudly, "I think I see where you are going with this."

All eyes. On me.

She marks something on my paper. "Sorry for my skepticism. I just didn't quite understand. . . . This is good. It's making me think. Very good. I'm glad to have you in my class." She hands me my paper without looking up. "You're bringing something different— not another year of testing the paper towel absorbencies. Speaking of which . . . Fred," she calls out, "I need to see you."

As I go to my seat, the kid she called up, Fred, passes me and winks. As I add *Other People's Awkwardness* to my brainstorming paper, Fred is telling Ms. Harding that he's heard that Brawny has given Bounty a run for its money and it's up to him to determine if this story holds water. Then he laughs. Ms. Harding laughs too. I add *puns* to my list. Ms. Harding tells him it's still a no, and she expects the *real* question to be ready tomorrow.

We've only got fourteen minutes left in class and my page is mostly blank. Still in writing position, I lean forward, ready for the ideas to flow, but my mind is empty. I can't think of a hint of a humorous thing. Maybe I do need to change my project. Something more paper towels and less . . . impossible.

I put down my pencil and try imagining a world where I want to be here, in this classroom, in this school. A world where I am awesome. Like what if I hung out with the guy in the tall pink socks and the high tops? That combo should look stupid, right? But it doesn't. He's got on basketball shorts and one of those pull-sweat-away shirts. Everything he's wearing—the shoes, the socks, the shorts, the shirt—has a Nike swoosh on it. He's definitely a sports kid. Could I be a sports kid too? Who knows. I've done okay in P.E., but we've moved so much, I've never actually been on a team before.

So maybe I wouldn't hang out with him. Maybe the kid next to him. Even though she's a girl, she definitely suits me more than Sports Mania. She looks nervous, biting her thumbnail and constantly shifting in her chair. Maybe we could hang out and worry together.

Fred, the kid the teacher called up after me, is in his chair again, the last seat in the last row. He's sitting back, slouched and lanky. He's not even trying to do his work; instead, he's fiddling with some little piece of paper, folding it over and over, only stopping to study it before folding it again.

He seems like the kind of guy that's super easy to like. He's cool without ever trying. Of course he'd do an experiment with paper towels—he's got no reason to do one about being funny, he's got no reason to bend his brain and come up with an academic masterpiece.

As I'm watching, somebody tosses a folded piece of paper onto Fred's desk. He unfolds it, reads it, and then looks over at the tosser of the note—Sports Mania—and they both laugh. Trent and I used to be like that. Better than that even. Our class only had two people so we didn't have to pass notes. But nobody here knows that I'm note-passing worthy. Not until I crack the code. When I understand how to be funny, guys like Sports Mania will want to pass *me* notes. They'll want to be my friend and watch me instead of doing their work.

I'll be easy to like, too. It shouldn't be that hard, right? I mean, look what Fred and I already have in common (see Figure 6).

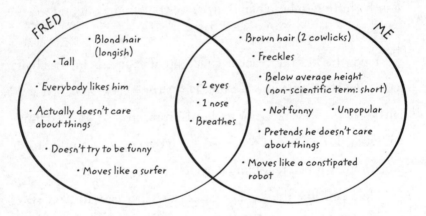

Figure 6. Venn diagram comparing Fred and me

Yup. When I'm funny, I'll have friends up to my eyeballs. And they'll be kids like Sports Mania and Fred. And we'll steer clear of the worrying girl and the kid in the row next to her who looks like he's got electrified hair. Seriously, his orangish-brown hair stands up a good three inches past where it should. But his oddness doesn't end there. He's like a study in the opposite of what I should be, with his too-short pants and his way-too-big black glasses that look like he stole them from his grandpa.

And shoot.

He caught me staring.

He's smiling at me.

I super fast smile back and then look at my desk until I'm sure he's not watching me anymore.

When I glance up again, the kid is still looking at me. He holds a finger up like he's telling me to wait, then he stands, pulls a cell phone out of his pocket, and holds it up in my direction. There's a clicking noise. He gives me a thumbs-up and sits again.

Wait.

Did he just take my picture?

I think he just took my picture.

I look at the teacher, since it is her job to protect us from the crazies. She's watching the phone kid. She waits until he's working again before she looks away. She doesn't say a word about what just happened. Sports Mania is the only person that reacts at all. He snickers. (Note for project: Sometimes people are laughing with you—but sometimes they are laughing at you. See Table 3.) If I'm going to be who I want to be here, I need to stay far, far away from the crazy-haired phone kid.

Table 3. Why Are They Laughing?

WHO	LAUGHING WITH	LAUGHING AT	NOTES	COMMENTS
Sports Mania	X		Athletic Sarcastic	Don't want to be on the punch line side of his jokes. Be his friend.
Fred	X		Cool Hair Cool Clothes Cool Everything	Old man name. Super chill. Everybody seems to like him (or at least nobody dislikes him).
Electric Hair		X	Crazy Hair Pants Too-Short Random Picture-Taker	What is wrong with this kid? Stay away.
Nail Biter		X	Bites Nails (which can give you worms) Rude	
Me	?	?	?	Not funny. At all.

LUNCH (AKA TORTURE to any kid that changes schools mid-year) is right after science. My normal strategy of lying low until the finale is not an option, if I listen to Trent. The Me, But Better does not sit quietly in a corner. Nope. The Better Me searches out the kids I want to be friends with and sits at their table so they recognize me as one of them.

After I get my lunch tray, I scan for Fred and Sports Mania. There's one seat left. It's next to the thumbnail biter from science. It's now or not at all.

"Can I sit here?" I ask when I get to the empty chair. But really it's not a question. I'm doing this. I set down my tray and start to pull out the chair.

The girl from science whips around and narrows her eyes like she just located her target. A voice in my head says, *Turn. Run. Nooowwww!!!!*

"That's Riley's seat," she snaps.

Aaaannnnnd of course somebody else would sit here. Now I feel like an idiot. "Cool. I didn't know." I shrug and start to back away.

Sports Mania from science is sitting on the other side of Seat-Saver and says, "Riley doesn't own it, Jenna. Chill."

"We can make room," says a girl that I haven't seen before. She puts her lunch box on the table where I'm not allowed to sit. "I heard about you. You're Ross, right?" She must be Riley, because Jenna doesn't freak out when her stuff touches the table.

I say yes, because I am Ross, even though I don't know what she's heard about me.

It seems to be the correct answer, because the Riley girl grabs a chair from the table behind us and slides it in next to Jenna. "You can sit here."

"Thanks." I force a smile and sit.

Everybody looks at me.

This is awkward.

I try to think of something to say but can't because the kids at the next table are glancing over and whispering. From their angry expressions, I don't think they're saying they want to come over and meet me.

I sit and try to block it out. I need to fit in at the table. But it's soooo hard with the glares.

Must. Ignore. Them. . . . Argh. This is hopeless.

I give up.

I'm about to return the chair as a peace offering, but the Seat-Saver girl, Jenna, beats me to a response. She scowls at the kids from the other table. "Do you have something you want to say?"

The silence that follows is painful. Everybody in hearing distance is suddenly and totally interested in their lunch—except for the girl holding her tray with nowhere to sit. She turns bright red. "No."

"Okay then." Jenna turns back around like she didn't just make everybody at both tables feel like they wanted to crawl beneath them. (Note for project: Some awkwardness is funny. Some is just awkward.)

"Jeez, Jenna," says Sports Mania.

Jenna shrugs. "If there is a problem, they should just say it."

I busy myself by arranging my tray so the points of the rectangle line up perfectly with the edge of the circular table. After I get it just so, I look up and realize Fred is watching me. I tap the right corner of the tray to mess it up so I don't look quite as crazy. I'm bringing my lunch from now on.

I pretend I don't care that Fred caught me being weird or that the girls behind me are sharing a seat since I'm sitting in the one stolen from them. I pretend I want to be right here eating my lunch because I'm a kid that belongs here. So, I take the Biggest Ever Bite of cafeteria pizza right as Fred asks, "Where'd you move from?"

Oh man.

No way I can answer. My mouth is too full.

I hold my finger up while I chew.

And chew.

And chew.

This pizza is made out of gum.

Why did I think it was a good idea to take a bite of pizza eligible to be recorded in the *Guinness Book of World Records?* (see Figure 7).

"Dude, you okay?" asks Sports Mania. Then he says, "I'm Justin, by the way."

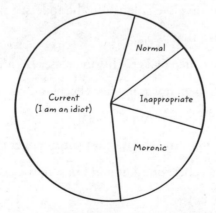

Figure 7. Explanation of bites of pizza

I raise my hand to wave and then cover my mouth in case I have any leftover pizza bits as I answer Fred's question. "I came from Boyett. It's in Louisiana."

"Why did you move?" asks Jenna.

"Had to," I say.

"Why?" Riley asks.

And maybe it was the way she said it—like a challenge. Or maybe I saw this as my chance to claim my spot. To be the funny guy. To start my legend. To be Me, But Better.

I shrug. "Suspension."

Sports Mania/Justin sits up straighter. I swear everybody looks at me like I suddenly matter.

"I have this thing I do. It's pretty funny. It's just teachers don't always like it."

Justin squints at me. "Like what?"

I shrug. "Putting live goldfish in the toilets. Salt in the coffee makers. Stuff like that."

"Salt in the coffee maker?" Justin crosses his arms.

"Yup. I told them it was my tears because I was leaving. Three teachers spewed that morning."

Well, only one. And she was just getting over the flu, anyway. But two other teachers drank it and I'm sure they gagged. I mean, how could they not?

Riley wrinkles her nose. "Gross!"

"Greatness," Fred says, and I smile, like *really* smile, for the first time since Mom told me we were staying. See? That's what being funny does for me.

"The goldfish one was even better," I say. I don't want to brag, but if they are going to know about my Exit-lence anyway, they definitely need to know about the best one to date. "I put a goldfish in every toilet. They were going to flush them, but kindergarteners were crying about it. The kids had to pee outside until the janitor scooped them out."

"Sounds epic," Fred says.

"Sounds rude and attention-seeking," Jenna sniffs.

Well, that was a mixed reaction. My ears burn. Riley leans toward me. I squeeze my hands into fists beneath the table. She's about to tell me I'm an idiot. This is going to backfire.

With a whisper loud enough for everyone to hear, she says, "Jenna's got a thing about truth."

"Not everybody is lucky enough to know how to lie," Jenna says. "I'm trying to make it even."

Sports Mania/Justin closes his eyes and holds his hands out like a zombie. "Since some people are blind, should we all walk around with our eyes closed?" he says, and swings around until he knocks Jenna's lunch box off the table.

"Jerk," she says.

Justin ignores her and leans toward me. "How many times have you moved?"

"Eleven."

His eyes get huge and he smiles. "So this will be twelve." He glances around like he's making sure the other tables aren't listening, "What are you planning when you leave here?"

I shrug. "Not sure." I shove in another bite of pizza so I don't have to talk.

Justin winks at me. "Nah, the way you say that doesn't have me convinced. I think you're just trying to throw us off so we don't see it coming. I respect that."

I smile, trying to look like I'm up to something. Or like I'm not going to talk about it. Because I can't. Talk, that is. Because I'm still chewing. Stupid gum-pizza.

"It's weird that you move so much," Jenna says.

"Hey, Jenna. Should we all move since Ross has to move all the time?" Justin asks.

"I wish you would," she says.

POPS IS IN his new place now. It is a lot less hospital-y, but it's still really smelly and uncomfortable. I don't think Pops likes it either, because whenever we come to visit, he's always just staring at the blank TV.

"Daddy," Mom says, walking in first. She straightens his pillows and grabs the remote. "Are you okay? Do you want me to turn this on?"

He turns toward her and the asleep-with-his-eyes-open expression goes away. He smiles and says, "No."

Then he rolls his head a little more so he can see around her. He raises his hand to wave at me. I raise mine back and tell him hello. Then, still looking at me, he slowly pats his bed and says, "Sit." Mom nods at me—I don't know if she's telling me that it is *okay* to listen, or that I *need* to listen, but either way, I settle as carefully as I can next to him.

His skin is so much less gray than it was when we got here a week ago, but his bruise is still an angry purple mask beneath his eyes and over his nose. When he slept so much last week, I could stare at it without him knowing. Now every time I turn to talk to him, I try to look him in the eyes instead of the bruise, but it's so hard. My eyes keep wandering to the purple and then I feel bad so I look away. Then I realize I'm avoiding him so I look him in the eyes again, and then I accidentally find the purple again and I look away. This continues. Basically, I'm caught in a cycle of being the world's worst grandson.

"So," he says—he's talking now. His words are slow and tired, but they are there. "I . . . have . . . a . . . bruise . . . on my face."

Mom stands up and walks over to him. "Yes, you do, Daddy. You fell last week. You had to go the hospital and now you're in an inpatient rehab facility to get you all better."

I swear he does this mini-eye roll—but he could just be fighting sleep. "I . . . know . . . that."

Mom's not bothered by his reaction—probably in part because the nurses, doctors, and physical therapists all said it's not uncommon to have a slight personality change as he heals or because he's always been a little grumpy anyway.

"Daddy," Mom says, loud and slow, "Ross had a good day at school today."

Pops looks at me. "Did you?"

I nod. Mom says, "Tell him about it."

I force myself to look at him while I'm speaking. When I can't concentrate on both focusing on his eyes and talking, I let my eyes study his bruise so I can concentrate on my words making sense.

He acts like he's listening as I tell him about my schedule and my teachers. He nods when I tell him it seems like an okay school. He only falls asleep for about two seconds—and honestly, I'm telling him about all the most boring stuff ever, so I don't blame him.

When I don't really know what else to say, I look at my hands and rub at a pen mark on my palm.

Pops coughs and then says, "Ross?"

"Yeah?" I say. I'm surprised he used my name. They said he might not remember.

"Does my face . . . still look . . . weird?"

"You look fine," I say.

"Don't lie," he says.

I look at Mom and she nods.

"It's not bad. But yeah, you look a little weird."

He nods. Two slow movements that make his face tight with effort. "That . . . makes . . . two of us."

From: nomadman@nma.com
To: herecomeztreble@nma.com
Subject: Mission Accepted

Yo T—

Operation: Be a Better Ross has begun. By the time I leave here, I will be somebody. A somebody that understands how to pull off the Best Exit Ever. All thanks to your tute-lage (I still love Mr. Bob for teaching us that word). You are my official tutor. Send any and all help my way.

Ross

— — — — — — — — — — — — —

From: herecomeztreble@nma.com
To: nomadman@nma.com
Subject: Re: Mission Accepted

Ross,

Tutelage is a good word, but dilapidated might have been my favorite Mr. Bob-ism. This is exciting. I've never had a student of my own before.

Let's see. As a good teacher I'd have to say . . . Sit up straight! Elbows off the table! Don't talk back to me, young man!

I could get used to this.

Mr. T

RESEARCH THE PROBLEM

Identify what you already know about this problem or question. What do you need to find out? What research needs to be done?

I CHECK AND recheck the zipper on my backpack as Mom is taking me to school. I want to make sure everything stays in place. And by "everything," I mean the research for my science project. Last night I flipped past the Exit-lence plans in my notebook and started writing my science project notes. My research is awesome. I watched four TV shows and took notes on everything that got a laugh. I also recopied my few measly brainstorming notes from class. Altogether, I have seven pages of solid research.

The first bell already rang. I hurry to my locker, pretending I'm in a rush so nobody notices my lack of a group and/or friends. It is one of the realities of new-kid-ness. The trick to overcome this, I've learned, is to pretend you don't stand out as much as a flea on a naked mole rat. Except that won't make a Me, But Better.

I need to be more. So when I see Fred at his locker, I make myself stop and say hi.

"Hey," Fred says back.

He doesn't seem bothered that I'm talking to him. This is good.

"So . . ." I'm about to say something about the homework, but then it occurs to me: *I could be funny right now.* Last night on the sitcoms I saw that funny people are always funny. Like Pops is always ready, even when he can barely talk. I've got to always be on, ready with a one-liner or some witty comment about the conversation.

"Yeah?" Fred pauses and looks at me, waiting.

This is my chance. I try to speak. I open my mouth to say a joke, but all that comes out is, "Um."

I can't think of anything. My mind is blank. This is ridiculous. I have pages and pages of TV show lines and irony and slapstick humor in my notebook, and short of slamming my own hand in his locker and pulling it out cartoon-style flat, only the horrible jokes my mom told me pop into my head (see Figure 8).

"Never mind."

Fred shrugs and reaches down for another book and I know it's time to bail. I've lost the moment. (Not like *just slipped by.* "Lost" as in *completely failed to win.*)

I force myself to swallow and unclench my hands, which I now realize are death-gripped to my backpack. "So, I'll see you around."

Fred winks as he walks away. It's a pity-wink. Like a

sympathetic pat on the head you'd give an ugly kid as you assure him he'll grow into his teeth someday.

Figure 8. Terrible Mom jokes

"Right, so . . . ," I say like I'm not currently standing by myself, then turn and walk away.

Stupid. Stupid. Stupid.

Why did I even stop? I undid everything I may have gained yesterday.

I want to bang my head against my locker. I'm such an idiot.

Proving myself right, I get my locker combo wrong on the first try. And on the second. And third.

For the fourth try, I put my backpack on the ground and square up to the lock and try again. It opens.

Okay, I tell myself as I pull out my math book, *I shouldn't be nervous. I've got pages of funny. They're already impressed by my Exit-lence. I can do this.*

As I close my locker and spin the dial, I mentally review more of the stuff I learned last night: Canned jokes are too forced and the perfect one-liners seem spontaneous.

But maybe I could have a couple of "spontaneous" comebacks ready. Like a pun or something. Like Fred used the other day with the paper towels. Like if somebody says "sense," I can pretend I thought he meant "cents." Like if somebody says, "He's got no sense!" And then I say, "Yeah, maybe he should go to the bank and get some." It's reaching—but I'm getting closer. Warming up. I'll get there.

I'm feeling better by the time I get to math.

My stomach squeezes from excitement, like when I solve a hard math problem; it's pleasant at first, but by the time the bell rings it's turned into an uncomfortable churning.

It's probably because there's a very small chance somebody will say "sense" out of the blue. But I can work around that. I can use it as a one-liner, like, "That teacher ain't got enough sense to make a dollar."

That's it! I can use that! It's hilarious! Or at least very sort of funny!

Success!

I know I need to write it down before I forget, because for me spontaneous doesn't happen without a well-thought-out plan. I reach for my backpack to get my notebook. And I uncover the real reason my stomach is twisting: Subconsciously I must have known that I NEVER PICKED UP MY BAG FROM THE FLOOR. My bag full of my stuff. My stuff that includes my notebook.

Oh no.

No. No. NO!

It's fine. It'll be fine, I tell myself in a calming voice like my mom used when I fell out of the moving truck and had to get six staples in the back of my head. *Everything will be ooooookay.*

The voice inside my head snaps and changes. *It's not fine, you dummy! Your notebook is out there. Unprotected! Unsafe! Anybody could walk by—they'll see the backpack and wonder whose it is and they'll open it to check and see the stupid notebook. You're toast, Moron.*

Why, oh why, didn't I let my mom monogram my backpack like she wanted?

Because a named sewed on your backpack is dumb, that's why! The voice screams.

I can fix this. I have to tell the teacher I need to go to the bathroom. Except this guy doesn't ever let anybody leave. Ever. It's the first thing he told me when I met him and it's posted, like, seven different times on his bulletin boards.

I'll tell him I have stomach trouble. That it's an emergency. He'll have to let me go.

I feel a little wobbly as I make my way to the front where Mr. Longfellow is sitting at his desk. Without looking up, he snaps, "Why are you breathing on me when you are *clearly* supposed to be doing your warm-up at your desk?"

"Oh. Um . . . I have a question?" I make my eyes big and raise my eyebrows trying to communicate that I'm just the newbie: I'm harmless and clueless. He won't take his eyes off his desk. I have no choice but to tell him about the fictional diarrhea, but it comes out as, "Um, I just . . . can I . . . uh . . ." My words fail. My heart is beating too fast.

"Um, uh, what?" He slams his red pen down and looks up and sees me with my scared-new-kid expression.

He jumps slightly. "Young man, are you okay? Do you have a problem? Medical or"—he leans forward—"*otherwise?*"

"No, I—"

He sits up. "Then you need to back up. You are invading my personal space."

He pushes his glasses up with one finger, picks up his red pen, and starts attacking the paper again. "In my class, you do *not* approach my desk without permission. You stay in your seat, raise your hand, and wait until you are called upon."

"Okay." I take a step back. "Do you, um, want me to do that now? For my question?"

Mr. Longfellow sighs and rolls his eyes. "What is your question?"

Say it now! Do it! But I cannot force the word "diarrhea" out of my mouth. Instead I say, "I think I left my backpack in the hall. Can I get it?"

He leans forward and starts marking with his red pen again, his strokes intentional as he writes an X. Then another. "If you cannot keep up with your belongings, that is your problem. You may not use *my* time to solve it."

"But I—"

He doesn't let me finish as he points to my seat.

I turn and shuffle back to my chair. My face is burning. So are my eyes. I squeeze them tight, but the sting doesn't go away. If I cry, I don't care what I promised Mom, I'm out of here.

I sit in my desk and realize that not only is my Exit-lence-Turned-Operation: Funny Notebook in my backpack, but so are my pencil and paper.

And just when I'm pretty sure I am definitely going to

bawl

or throw up

or pass out

or all of the above,

My prayers are answered in the form of the mildly rude, thumbnail-biting, truth-obsessed girl from the cafeteria. Jenna walks through the door holding a small pink paper in one hand and my bag in the other.

Mr. Longfellow doesn't even glance up as she sets the pass on the corner of his desk. Jenna turns and glances over the rows, spots me, and holds up the backpack like she's checking if it is mine.

I nod so hard—my backpack is like an oxygen tank and I'm in a drowning sea self-stupidity. Stone-faced and purposeful, she walks to my desk and holds it out to me.

My fingers clutch the blessed canvas and I hold the bag to my chest. I stop myself short of nuzzling it.

Relief floods me and fat teardrops of joy threaten to flood out—but those are much easier to hold back. I smile really big and even offer a thumbs-up so she knows how grateful I am. She nods seriously, accepting my thanks.

I check the bag for my notebook.

It's there!

My happiness is immediate. All-consuming . . . short-lived.

She may have seen that notebook.

I repeat: The truth-above-all-else girl MAY HAVE SEEN THE NOTEBOOK.

She may have seen everything I wrote in there. She may have seen everything I wrote about *everyone else* in there.

Again, I must say: OH. NO.

I replay our interaction and try to read her expression. Her lack of emotion gives me nothing.

Nothing. Nada. Zip. Zilch.

I could just ask her—I know she'll tell me the truth.

But that'd be like giving myself a wedgie in a crowded hallway. Like stuffing spinach in my teeth and then smiling. And carrying around a dumb notebook about how to be funny already makes me look like an idiot (see Table 4).

Table 4. Levels of Idiotism

6	Walking around with toilet paper stuck to your shoe
5	Leaving your zipper down
4	Calling your mom "mommy"
3	Calling your mom "mommy" in public
2	Eating your boogers (in public or not)
1	Keeping a How-to-be-Funny notebook full of incriminating notes

I'm still in crisis mode when Mr. Longfellow finally ambles up to the front and drones on about multiplying fractions. Instead of listening, I spend the next twenty minutes trying to come up with ways to ask Jenna if she saw the notebook without actually asking her.

Before he sits down, Mr. Longfellow writes the assignment on the board. Everybody around me flips to that page in their book.

I force myself to follow suit and attempt to distract myself by starting the work, but I can't focus. Even with pencil and paper, I'm going to fail this assignment.

Of course I am. It just matches the rest of my day.

No, not just my day.

Nothing has gone right from the moment I left my last school. I'm in over my head. There's no way I can do this. We're here indefinitely, I can't figure out how to find my funny, and without that I've got nothing.

Apparently, by science I've looked at Jenna enough that I'm raising suspicion.

She's started glancing back at me and turns a bright red if she catches my eye. Justin's asked twice if I *like* like her. And even though Riley is in another class, when I saw her in the hall between classes, she stopped in front of me, crossed her arms as if my very existence made her unhappy, and said, "So you like Jenna, huh?"

I've sworn to Justin, Riley, and about twelve other kids that I don't *like* like anybody.

I don't know why they even keep asking me. Even if I am new to the school, it's a universal rule at any school to deny any and all crushes (see Table 3). So I wouldn't tell them even if I did like Jenna—which I *don't*.

I'm trying (and failing) to focus on what Ms. Harding is

Table 5. Universal Rules of Seventh Grade Survival

1	You can like school—but not too much.
2	You can get excited about stuff—but not too much.
3	It's best to only moderately care about anything.
4	Rules 2 and 3 do not pertain to sports.
5	Rules 2 and 3 do not apply if you are a prodigy (at least good enough for the local news).
6	Never ever, ever admit to, like, liking somebody (unless everybody else admits to liking them too and/or they were on the local news).
7	Understand your parent(s)/guardians(s) have blocked out all memories of actually being a student due to PTSD (post-traumatic school disorder).

saying. I've missed the entire first part of her lecture and tune back in time to hear, "Your peer reviewer is the first person you go to if you have a question or problem. If you *both* don't know that answer then you can ask me. Since your partners are also doing a project, they should be an expert on the scientific process."

"Especially me," says this kid named Brady, and everybody laughs. From the way he sleeps through class, I'm guessing it's only funny because it's the opposite of true.

Knowing my luck lately, I'll be assigned to him.

I cross my fingers, toes, and eyes and wish to be partnered with Fred, but that hope is crushed when he's immediately partnered with some girl named Chloe. My name is called and I'm matched with somebody named Peter.

Ms. Harding finishes and gives us the go-ahead to split. I stay in my chair and wait for whoever I'm paired with to find me, since I have no idea who Peter is. Everybody's moving around, grouping off. Some kid is walking toward me and I think he wouldn't be so bad, but he passes right by. Just when I think my partner must be absent, the electricity-eating kid comes up to my desk and says, "I'm Peter." He holds out his hand like we're adults.

"I'm Ross," I say, pausing before I accept the handshake.

"We're partners. I need to get a picture." He doesn't wait for me to answer. He lines up next to me and holds out his phone. It's all done before I can say no or even smile.

"I want to show my dad who I'm working with," he says, like that makes it any less weird.

So this is my partner. Great.

I scan the room hoping there's a second Peter roaming around and this one has come up to me by mistake.

Everybody else is already hunkered down and talking—except for Chloe, who is red-faced and grinning like a maniac. Fred is studying a scab on his knee and doesn't seem to notice her sneaking glances at him.

"Should we go sit somewhere?" he asks.

"Okay," I say. "But no more pictures."

He looks at me like I'm the crazy one. "Why would I take more pictures?"

"Right." Yeah, I'm the weird one. I grab my stuff and tell Partner Peter to lead the way.

He walks to the back corner of the classroom and moves a trash can so we have room to sit on the floor. He doesn't notice all the dust bunnies as he plops down right on top of them.

He waits for me to sit, then pushes up his gigantic glasses and says, "So what's your project about?"

I smile like I'm not wishing I had any other partner besides him (with the exception of that Chloe girl) and say, "Let's do yours first."

He leans back against the wall, crushing his insane hair. "Do you like video games?" he asks.

"I guess."

"What's your favorite one?"

"I don't know."

He pushes up his glasses again. "Minecraft? Mario Kart? Or something old school like Pokémon or Zelda?"

"I don't know."

"When I play games like that, or watch scary movies, I get this . . . I don't know . . . feeling." He pats his chest. "My heart starts beating fast. My mouth gets dry. I don't even notice if I'm hungry or not. Sometimes it makes me feel like I have to pee."

"Aren't we supposed to be talking about our project?" (Actually, I take it back. Chloe would be fine too.)

Maybe if I pull the new-kid card Ms. Harding will put me with another partner. Maybe she'll put me with Fred, since Chloe obviously needs to be moved away from him in order to relearn the English language. I watch them to gather evidence to present to Ms. Harding. Chloe has yet to speak. She's arranging and rearranging her papers on her desk. Fred's drawing something on the leg of his jeans.

Then I realize Peter's still talking. ". . . flight, you know? I want to know what'll happen." He stops. I think he wants me to respond. He's staring at me, waiting. All I can think is: *You've got really poofy hair.*

"Yeah. I get it," I say. Except I don't. I don't even have a clue what he said. All I heard was sometimes he has to pee and "flight." I'm about to ask him to repeat it, but he leans forward and starts speaking again before I can.

"And what do you think they'll do?" he asks.

"Um, no idea."

"So"—the sides of his mouth keep twitching and he shrugs like he is trying to pretend that he's not as excited about whatever he's excited about—"that's the experiment. Cool, huh?"

I nod even though I have no clue what he said.

He leans back into the corner like he's exhausted from all the excitement. His hair touches both walls. He pushes up his glasses. "What's yours?"

I don't want to tell him. I don't want anything to do with him. Plus, I refuse to talk about my project out loud.

I picture myself telling him. Then I picture his face, him rolling his eyes and laughing at me. Not that I care what this kid thinks, but still. . . .

Actually, I don't even need to explain my project. By the time this thing is due, I'll be long gone. Pops gets so much better every day. I'd bet in the next couple of weeks we can even make it to the end of St. Louis.

I just need something to say I'm doing in the meantime . . . a place filler. "Paper towels," I blurt out. "I'm going to see which one is the most absorbent."

Peter frowns.

"You know Brawny has been saying they're better," I say, borrowing Fred's joke. "I want to see if that holds water."

Peter scratches his cheek, then glances at Fred and back to me. "Um. Okay. That's sounds . . . well, I have more ideas. I can help you come up with a different one if you want."

Irritation jolts me. Who does this kid think he is? Telling me what he thinks I should or shouldn't do. And plus, that's not even my *real* project. I'm not a moron. Well, neither is Fred—he's just laid-back and stuff.

I narrow my eyes at this Peter kid. "I like the paper towel project," I say.

"Okay," he nods hard. His hair is on a two-second delay. "Sure. It is a good one." He writes "Paper Towel Project" in his notebook. "It's been around forever. How can it be wrong?"

I can't tell if he's being sarcastic or not, but the thing is, I don't care. I'm not worried about what Peter thinks about me. He's not part of the Me, But Better plan.

It's weird, because since I'm not worried about Peter I feel okay—brave even—so I decide to give my one-liner a try. For the sake of my experiment.

I nod my head in the direction of Chloe and Fred. Chloe finally seems to be making progress. She's only cotton-candy pink now and her mouth is finally moving, but from here I can't be sure that actual words are coming out. "That Chloe girl seems to be having a hard time."

I give Peter a second to study her. "Yeah, she looks . . . flustered. She's really nice though." He turns more so he can look at her. "When she's nervous, she stutters some. Do you think we—"

I'm losing his attention. My chance is slipping. I interrupt him. "Yeah. When we leave class she'd better stop by the bank."

Peter turns his attention back to me. "The bank?"

I nod. "Yup. That girl needs to get some sense."

Peter smiles. He laughs. Barely. But still. I did it. I was funny. Sort of.

From: herecomeztreble@nma.com

To: nomadman@nma.com

Subject: Mr. Bob would be so proud.

> Yes! Your equation is perfect. There is never a time that funny is not awesome.
>
> You are so lucky! I wish I had me to tell me how to do this when I moved here.
>
> Your Teacher,
> Mr. T

LIST THE MATERIALS YOU WILL USE

What do you need to complete your investigation?

IN MY NOTEBOOK, I have

Jokes

One-liners

Gestures

Observations

Anything and everything funny

Peter's laugh and Trent's e-mail showed me I want to be funny.
I *need* to be funny.

But Mom and I must be like an hourglass where if one side fills
up, the other empties out, because she seems like she's lost a little
of her happy.

We're sitting in the living room and watching a pretty hilarious movie about a family vacation where everything goes wrong.

Every time I laugh, I glance over at Mom to see if she is too, and she's staring off into space.

"Mom?" I say when I find that I'm starting to miss all the jokes in the movie because I'm too busy watching her watch nothing.

"Hmmm?" she says as a reflex. Her eyes, eventually, focus on me.

"You okay?" I ask.

She bites her bottom lip.

Lip biting is very, very bad. It trumps whatever words she says.

"I am," she says and then chomps down some more.

"We can play a game or something if you don't want to watch this show," I offer.

"Oh, no," she shakes her head, "the show's good. I'm really enjoying it."

I let her lie slide and don't point out that she's not even paying attention to it. I briefly consider offering to do a puzzle with her, but I'm not that desperate yet. I scan my brain to think of something else she always wants to do. "What about a walk? The weather's nice today."

She nods absent-mindedly. She doesn't even notice that I'm willingly offering to go on a walk instead of watch a movie. This is bad. Now nervousness is sneaking into my stomach. I want to ask her more—to find out what is wrong—but I also sort of don't want to know. Sometimes she gets upset about stuff that just works out.

Or it doesn't, but I can't help other than doing stuff like picking walks over movies. And I'm really trying not to think about it, but maybe something's wrong with Pops. He seems better every time we visit him, but he's definitely not all the way better yet.

"Mom?"

"Hmmm," she says like she's only now realizing I spoke again.

"A walk? Want to go on one?"

She looks at the front door and frowns, but then turns back to me and changes her expression to Happy Mom. Her face is like those happy/sad masks you see on theater buildings. "Sure. That's a great idea. That'd be great."

We both grab our shoes and jackets. Outside the wind bites my cheeks and the cold stings the inside of my nose, but it's still nice to be somewhere other than school or the house or the hospital.

Pops's house is really nice—much better than the other houses and apartments we've stayed in—and even though the neighborhood is repetitive (bad when you are running away from school), it's tidy and cozy with all its brick and neat front yards. Plus, it's also a just-right distance from the city. Cities always have cool stuff to do—museums, restaurants, water parks—but they also feel busy and grumpy. But if you get too far away the houses are too big, the yards are too small, and everybody has a perfect home and a perfect family: a mother, father, sisters, and/or brothers. My mom and I are a basket of food and a dad short of a family picnic.

I don't need a brother or sister or a dad. Mom and I are fine. Better than fine. We're a team, an ensemble. She watches after me and I watch after her. And Pops is our biggest fan; he's our groupie. Until last year when he had a little heart scare, he'd come see us in every place we toured.

Neither Mom or I speak as we walk. By the time we get to the street that dead ends at the school, mom's lip chewing has stopped. Maybe she just needed a little break. A little fresh air. My shoulders relax. I don't realize how stressed I am until I'm not.

"This really is a nice neighborhood, isn't it?" Mom asks, and shifts her lip back into pre-bite position as she waits for my answer. This makes it seem like more than just passing conversation. Like my answer actually matters.

I shrug. "Yeah."

"And you're liking the school? Making friends?"

I give her truth on credit. Once I figure out the funny, life will be perfect. "Yeah. I'm getting to know people."

She's quiet again.

"Mom?"

"Yeah?"

"Why?"

She shrugs. "I've just been thinking. . . ." I hold my breath waiting for her to tell me what's next because I know it'll be important. If my life had a soundtrack, this would be part that goes

DUN-DUN-DUUUNNNNN. She never finishes her sentence. Instead she pauses and says, "Do you know them?" and points to the open part of the playground where some kids are practicing soccer. Well, actually, they're not kids, they're girls. Girls in my grade.

"Yeah." I recognize Jenna, Riley, Macy, and several others whose names I can't quite remember yet. "They're in my grade."

Mom nods. Then, even with this knowledge, she stays on the sidewalk that goes around the outside edge of the school. If we follow this path, we'll have to pass right by them (see Figure 9). Which is, of course, a terrible idea. Because they will see me. With my mom. And Jenna is there. And she could have seen the notebook. And there is not a seventh grader on the planet that would think it's a good idea for the new kid to stroll by all the girls in his class (including one that could easily blackmail you) with his mom. Clearly Mom's never had proper parent training to minimize kid embarrassment.

I try to keep the panic out of my voice as I say, "You know what? Let's turn here. I want to see more of the neighborhood."

"I like this path," she answers.

"Cool," I say, and pretend it is so I don't make her suspicious. For a few minutes we can't see the soccer girls because the school is between them and us.

I attempt Diversion Tactic Two. "Let's turn around and go back home. We can do a puzzle together. Any one you want."

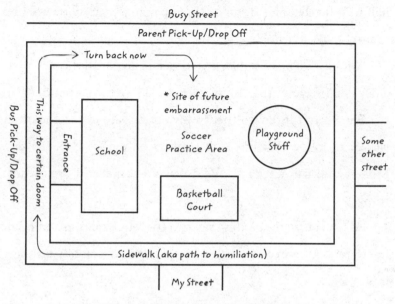

Figure 9. Future site of certain doom

She nods. "That sounds fun. We'll do that after our walk."

Great. Imminent humiliation directly followed by putting together a thousand-piece puzzle of sailboats. What have I done to deserve this?

One more attempt. Something she can't dodge. My tried and true method. And since it is my mom (instead of my teacher), I'll be able to commit to the act. "I think I need to go back. I've got to go to the bathroom. The pizza isn't sitting well." I hold my stomach and moan to give her a visual.

She pauses and I think I've won, but then she gives me a suspicious look. "You were fine a few minutes ago. We're already half way. It's the same distance to keep going." She starts walking again. I hurry to catch up.

"Mom." We make it past the corner. I can see all the girls now. They don't see me. Yet. "Mom, *please*. Can we turn around?"

She doesn't listen. In theory, my options are to run the other way or to follow her. But realistically I only have one. If I ran, Mom would call after me. We'd make a scene; it'd be a whole thing.

All the girls are standing next to the fence talking and holding water bottles even though none of them are actually drinking from them.

"Mom," I whisper, hoping she'll hear the pleading in my voice, "keep walking. Act like you don't see them."

"Why?" Mom whispers way too loudly back. "I think that'd be too obvious. Just play it cool."

Right.

You know what's not cool? When your mother says, "Play it cool."

Also not cool: passing by all the girls in your grade with said mom beside you.

I speed up, keeping my face forward, my eyes focused down on the sidewalk. Mom keeps up beside me. From my peripheral vision and my strained hearing, I can tell the girls haven't noticed us yet, which means they haven't given Mom an opening. This is good. Just a little farther and—

"Aren't you going to say hi to your friends?" Mom says. Loudly.

I freeze. Only a couple of girls look over at us. Maybe I can still save the situation.

I thread my arm through my mom's and try to pull her along. "They're in the middle of practice, *Mom*," I say with gritted teeth. "We don't want to bug them."

"I'd like to meet the other parents," she whispers back. Then my mom does, like, the most embarrassing thing ever. She walks over to her fence, holds her hand out the way Peter did in science, and says, "Hi. Ross says you're in his class. I'm his mother, Christa."

Every girl from my grade turns toward her like they are controlled by one brain.

None of them move. They look at my mom, at her outstretched hand, and then at me. I do my best version of oh-hey-what-are-you-doing-here-I-totally-didn't-see you.

Still nobody moves. And because this moment is not horrible enough, suddenly a little boy runs up, grabs the chain-link fence, shakes it making it rattle against the posts. And he screams, "Stranger! Stranger Danger! Daddy! Jenna! Stranger Danger!"

Now.

This exact moment would be the perfect time to say something funny. Or to spontaneously combust. But funny sounds better. And less messy.

Right *now.*

I could fix this with *one joke.*

But my brain can't even function enough to pull my mom away from the fence or to tell that kid that he should probably stop screaming before he passes out.

Maybe I should run instead. Leave her behind. Every mom for herself.

"Stranger!" The kid screams. Then Jenna is there, picking him up and saying, "No, Toby. They aren't strangers. I know them. They're my friends."

"No . . . I . . . I'm sorry. I didn't mean to . . . ," Mom says, and she starts to pull her hand back, like she suddenly realizes what a horribly embarrassing, terrible idea this was.

Just before Mom's finished bringing all her appendages to our side, a hand grabs hers.

"I'm Joel," the man attached to the hand yells so we can hear him over the screaming kid. "I'm Riley's dad. Girls, don't be rude. Come meet . . . uh . . . what did you say your name was again?"

Mom looks flustered, but finally yells back, "Christa. I'm Ross's mom. We've just moved here."

And the world's most painfully earned handshake ends.

"Um, I'm sorry. I didn't mean—" She gestures at the scream-ing kid.

"Oh," the guy waves his hand like he's batting away her words. "Don't worry about Toby. He just learned about Stranger Danger and is taking it very seriously." He winks.

Mom frowns, but quickly recovers her smile as the parents come toward us. She doesn't offer her hand again. At least she's a quick learner.

The boy's yells reach a new level of ear-splitness. Another man has picked him up out of Jenna's arms. The boy, Toby, is try-ing to wriggle out of his grip while still pointing and staring at Mom and me with wild, scared eyes. Jenna's watching him with the same expression I saw her make when she got a question wrong in social studies. But here at the fence, everybody ignores the man and Toby and Jenna.

More people want to talk to us—all the parents. A line has formed and suddenly we're meeting a ton of people, the parents are talking about adding Mom to e-mail lists and telling her about upcoming birthday parties, all while the boy behind them is screaming his head off and Jenna and the man—her dad?—look like they need help.

I'm trying really hard to ignore it like everybody else, but in a moment of weakness, I glance over again and find Jenna looking at me. She has a sudden and intense interest in the ground in front of her, and I realize how stupid I am. I've been feeling sorry for *her*, when I bet she's probably feeling sorry for *me*. Jenna could be embarrassed, I guess, but the data suggests it's more likely I'm the reason (see Figure 10).

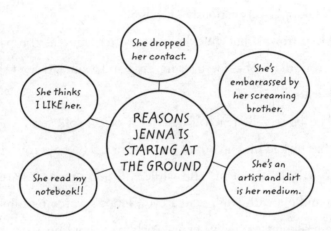

Figure 10. Reasons Jenna is staring at the ground

We need to go. Now.

We need to break away from this crowd that has formed to meet my mother. Either she's better at this friend thing than me or they're just here to get intel so they can accurately make fun of us when we leave.

I nudge Mom, just barely, with my elbow. Thankfully, she finally gets it. She tells our audience it's getting dark, that we need to get home and we need to eat dinner (even though only the first one is true).

When we're back on the path, Mom is smiling. I am not. I feel as heavy as if I had already eaten the second dinner Mom lied about.

"I hope Toby's okay," Mom says and glances back at everybody.

"Me too."

"I guess he does that a lot?"

I shrug. I don't want a conversation. I just want to be back at the house. "I don't know."

"That was really nice to meet some other people. I needed that. Thanks for suggesting a walk. I feel a lot better."

I nod and try to be happy that Mom seems happy, but my mind is a jumble of sick grandfathers and weird science partners and funniness failures and screaming kids and notebooks that may or may not have been read.

"Ross?" Mom, says interrupting my trip down Unpleasant Memory Lane. "Pops is coming home soon."

This is the best news I've heard all night. All week. All year.

So why does Mom look so worried?

"But he still needs us. We can't just leave him. Not when he needs us, can we?"

Is there any way I could say we should leave? "I guess not."

"And . . . ," she starts as she turns the key in the lock to open the front door. Her back is to me so I can't see her face. "I've accepted a substitute position at the high school. Just temporarily. To teach music."

"Okay," is all I can think to say.

She opens the door. "I love you?"

I force a smile because the hourglass has tipped and it's her turn to be happy. "I love you too," I say as I walk inside.

She sets the keys on the moving boxes labeled "Misc." that we've stacked in the entryway.

I force another version of a Happy Face and then sit in the same place I was in before the walk and pick a sitcom instead of the movie.

The laugh track on the television makes me reach for my notebook. I turn to the next clean page, then rewind the show and play it again so I can hear what was so funny. I watch the entire thing, paying close attention to the jokes, but nothing makes me laugh.

WHEN WE GET to Pops's room, he's sitting up a chair and watching TV.

"Look at you!" Mom says when we walk in.

"Yes," Pops says. His voice is stronger this week. "I am . . . the best chair sitter . . . in all the world."

Mom rolls her eyes and leans down to kiss him on the cheek.

Pops leans up to let her and then he turns to me and smiles. "Hi, kid."

Mom frowns and says, "Dad, it's Ross."

Now it's Pops's turn to roll his eyes. They don't quite make a full circle, but he still makes his point. "I know that." He grips the sides of his chair. "Hey, Ross-kid . . . do you want to see something special?"

He doesn't wait for my answer as he grips the sides of his chair so hard, his knuckles turn white. He pushes off the chair arms, grunting. Mom hurries to him, putting her hand under his arm to help him. He pauses before he's upright and cuts his eyes to her. "I got this."

"Okay, okay. Sorry. I don't want you to fall again." She steps back and holds her hands up.

"I accept . . . ," he straightens up, "your apology." Then he walks, one slow foot in front of the other, toward the bed. His steps get longer as he goes. When he's almost there, he reaches for the bed, grabbing the rails as his knees bend too much. But he makes it.

He's breathing hard and his forehead is shiny from sweat. He sits on the bed and points to me. "Bet . . . you didn't . . . think . . . I could . . . do that." His hand falls to his knee as if holding it up is too much work. His chest and stomach are heaving. It's like his entire body is team dedicated to making him breathe.

He is watching me, waiting; I don't know what he's waiting

for exactly. Sympathy? Disappointment? Excitement? Because I'm feeling all three.

"How do you like me now?" he asks.

"Wow, Pops. That's pretty great," I say. I must have got it right because he nods and he's pressing his lips together like he's all I-told-you-so. Except I didn't even know it was a big deal. I mean, sure he hasn't been talking or walking, but he's been so tired. Lots of people stay in bed when they're sick. Then they get better and they stand up.

Mom helps him get his feet into the bed. He fights with her on whether or not he should she should cover him with a sheet. He tells her the sheets make him hot, and if they are on him, he can't get out of bed as easily, to which Mom says, "*Exactly.*"

I fake a laugh, so they think I think their argument is funny. I stuff my hands in my pockets so they can't see me squeezing my fists so tight my fingernails have got to be leaving marks on my skin.

From: nomadman@nma.com

To: herecomeztreble@nma.com

Subject: My Pops Could be a Liar

So "Mr. T,"

Help me with this one.

Today Mom and I went to visit Pops. He showed off by taking approximately two steps and almost collapsing. After we'd been there a while, they brought his dinner. He tried to eat, but he just kept trying and trying and no matter what, he couldn't get the food to his mouth. Which is weird. It's like you are a baby, then an adult, and then you grow back into a baby. Finally, he gave up and put his fork down and Mom asked if he wanted her to do it. He said yes.

So anyways, Mom FED Pops like he's a little baby. And then this nurse came in and Mom was all, "Did you know this poor man is STARVING?! He can't feed himself and you just throw food at him and run!" And the nurse said, "This guy?" like Mom could be talking about another person. Mom was like, "YES!" and she stands up and says, "Tell her how hungry you are, Daddy!" And then we all look at Pops and he's snoozing—sleeping as hard as humanly possible. And then the nurse and Mom just sort of looked at each other and I was so uncomfortable. So I said, "He probably passed out from lack of nutrition," which totally saved them from fighting. I should have been the hero. But I didn't count on Mom wanting to yell at somebody and she was like, "It's neither the time nor the place, Ross. Neither the time, nor the place."

It was so weird—I couldn't even be mad at her for it. You know and I know and she knows that she never talks to me like that. So of course she starts crying. So of course then I have to keep apologizing for her yelling at me.

And I SWEAR, when I glanced at Pops, his mouth was either spasming or he was trying not to smile. I'm starting to wonder if he's faking.

Ross

— — — — — — — — — — — — — — —

From: herecomeztreble@nma.com

To: nomadman@nma.com

Subject: Re: My Pops Could be a Liar

Dear Devoted Student,

That is a tricky one. I can think of several ways to determine if he is fake sleeping, but unfortunately, because your grandfather is elderly, they could end in heart attacks and they are not advised.

Time will tell, my little grasshopper, and lucky for you, time is what you need for your experiment. While we can't trust all the words of Mr. Bob, we can trust my coach since he regularly dominates life. His favorite saying is: Go Big or Go Home.

Go forth and be funny.

Mr. T

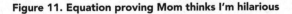

TEST YOUR HYPOTHESIS

Record and describe the observations

you made during your investigation.

TRENT IS RIGHT. Go big or go home. Since I don't have a home, I've got to go big.

It's Monday morning and I am ready. Sure, I felt knocked down for a bit, but it just motivated me. So we're going to be here longer than I thought. That's okay. I can handle it.

I watched extra-hilarious movies all Saturday. I practiced all Sunday when I visited Pops. I tried for hilariousness with Mom this morning. She smiled, which means I was awesome because she hadn't even had her coffee yet (see Figure 11).

Mom smiling + No coffee =
Peeing her pants from laughing

Figure 11. Equation proving Mom thinks I'm hilarious

I feel funny. I am funny. I can't be held back. I'm lighter. Sillier. Borderline giddy. I can see myself at this school, hour after hour, day after day until we get to go. This could even help my future Exit-lence. I won't just have one moment of glory—I'll have a legend.

So after painstaking research of hours of TV watching, it seems easy enough. Here is what I know:

IS IT:

A pun or play on words OR
Ironic OR
Slapstick/physical OR
A proven joke (not a mom one) OR
Mildly self-depricating OR
Different from expectation

Figure 12. Is it funny?

So yeah, I've totally got this.

First class. Math with Mr. Longfellow. We're still working on multiplying fractions. Hilarious stuff keeps popping into my head. Even though I can't say it out loud, everything is on the tip of my tongue waiting to spill out. Like when Mr. Longfellow finishes showing us how to set up the equation and asks, "Does everybody understand how to get the answer?" I picture myself leaning back and kicking my feet up on the desk across the row from me and saying, *I understand how to get the answer—if all the fractions multiplied by zero*, which is totally witty and self-deprecating (see Figure 12). But I keep it to myself because to speak out loud would be to risk his wrath, and then I might not live long enough to enjoy my triumph.

When he writes the assignment on the board, I almost, *almost* raise my hand and say, *How about we do a fraction of that work—* ironic, because this is a lesson about *fractions*, and I can make a pun (again, see Figure 12). I should say it. But the moment passes and it is too late. A future legend would have said it.

I'll have to take a chance. My mind is crouching like a cheetah ready to spring. I'll take my next opportunity and go for it. My stomach is squeezing; my heart is pounding.

Here I go.

"I understand this!"

Everybody turns to look at me, and I pause for effect before I add the punch line.

"Not even a little!"

Aaaannnnnd . . . everybody is still looking at me. Nobody is laughing.

Argh. It totally worked in my head. It should be funny: I insulted myself. I ended it with a surprise (see stupid Figure 12, again).

Why isn't anybody laughing?

"Well, I have after-school hours for tutoring," Mr. Longfellow says. "How about you come by and we'll also have a remedial lesson on how to raise your hand."

Sure, that gets a laugh.

And then it is over. People start working. Only Jenna is still staring at me, frowning. I can't tell if it's because she feels sorry for me or because she feels obligated to let me in on the fact that I'm an idiot. I bend over my paper and pretend to work. My ears are burning. My brain is unraveling. I'm such an unfunny moron.

SECOND PERIOD. OUR specials class today is P.E.

I'm pumping myself up. I've got this. I *can* be funny. I shouldn't worry about before—everybody stumbles on the way to greatness. That's what movies are made of. It's what the best stories are all about.

I'm doing it—I'm going BIG.

Today we're playing basketball. Plenty of self-deprecation opportunities for me here. There's only a tiny part of me that says, *Yeah, how'd that work last time?* And, *Mr. Longfellow got way more laughs than you.*

Coach Martin splits us up into four groups. We're using goals on the sides of the gym instead of full court so everybody can play at once. The boys are on one side and the girls are on the other.

I'm on a team with Fred and three guys I don't really know. We're playing against Justin's team.

Coach Martin blows the whistle and we're off. My entire attempt is like one big slapstick comedy routine—and not on purpose. I reach for the ball and totally miss it. I get the ball and then lose it. I get the ball and shoot it . . . it misses the rim and hits one of the girls.

I try to pretend to blow it off and say things like, "Oh, I was supposed to make it in the basket," or, "I totally meant to do that." But it's like they don't even hear me.

I shouldn't be surprised that Fred is so good at basketball, but I am. He seems like he'd be too chill to even care. He really is one of those people that has it so easy in life. Everything he touches turns to awesome.

No thanks to me, the score gets up to twenty-two to twenty, with our team in the lead. And by our team, I mean it is mainly Fred and we are lackeys. I personally support him best by attempting to *not* touch the ball at all, which is a boring but effective strategy for our team's victory.

Even though he's easily the best player on the other team, Justin doesn't look like he's having much fun either. His face is red and he keeps yelling at his teammates to get open or to pass to him. When Coach Martin calls out to say we only have two minutes left, Justin tips his head back and puffs out his cheeks.

I recognize this opportunity when I see it. Justin is frustrated and tense. Fred doesn't even really care. This game's not a big deal and if I play it right (my cards, not the game—that ship has sailed), I could break the tension and be the hero. I'd have to make a scene. I saw something like it on a TV show and it totally made me crack up. I'd have to make a sacrifice. It'd be awkward and embarrassing, but it'd *definitely* be funny.

At least a minute passes and I don't think I'm going to get my chance. The score is tied at twenty-four. But I need to make it happen because if we all tie, it's like everybody wins.

So, when Justin lines up to take a game-winning shot, I do it. I go BIG.

"*Bock*," I say once, loud enough to make Justin hesitate and pull the ball back.

He lines up to shoot again and I fully commit. I tuck my hands in my armpits so I have pretend wings and yell, "*Bock, bock, bock, boooooooock*," like a chicken. For a second everyone from both sides stops to look at me.

It's quiet and then—yes—some people are laughing! Some are just staring, but there are definitely a few chuckles in there! Victory is mine!

Right then the second-worst guy on my team yanks the ball out of Justin's hands. No amount of *bocking* can stop him. He's gone, (badly) dribbling down the court before Justin realizes what just happened. Still Justin tries to catch him, but with the small courts, the kid is already down there and he shoots. The ball swishes through the net.

"Yes!" Fred says. "We won!"

"That's not fair!" Justin says as he catches the ball and slams it down. "They cheated."

I'm still standing there, my arms still folded up like wings, when the coach blows her whistle. "There's no penalty in the rule book for acting like a bird." She laughs. "You chickens and children put up the balls, get changed, and get ready to go."

I ignore the fact that people are still watching me and I jog to get a ball and take it over to the rack. Maybe it's not as bad as I think. Surely Justin would think that was funny, right? Or at least he'd realize I didn't mean to make him lose. We are friends, right?

Maybe he's even bee-lining toward me to congratulate me on my creative basketballing.

"What the heck?" Justin says when he gets close, too close, to me. "That was a stupid thing to do."

"Bock?" I say and pick up a ball that has rolled up to my feet.

"I lost because of you and *whatever* that was."

It was funny, I want to say. "It was a good game."

"That was a cheap shot," he says and hits the ball in my hands to knock it down, then walks away.

Fred and the winning scorer for my team walk up and put some balls on the rack. "That was hilarious, man," Fred says.

"And the only time I'll ever score against Justin in my life," the other kid adds. "So thanks for that."

"Sure," I say, but I already know I've made a big mistake. Never thought going BIG would make me feel so small.

IN SCIENCE, I try to catch Justin's eye so I can smile at him, remind him we are friends, and we can put the whole stupid chicken thing behind us. He won't look at me. Ms. Harding makes us meet with our peer review partner again. Honestly, I still don't have a clue what Peter is working on. Something about animals, I think. He mentioned birds flying or something. I'll figure it out today.

"How are the paper towels?" he asks when we sit down in our corner.

"Rolls and rolls of fun," I say, and he gives me a forced smile. It only deflates me a little. "What about your, um, project?" I ask.

He takes a big irritated breath and for a second I'm worried about what's coming next. Considering I've been the World's Worst Partner, he's got plenty to be mad about.

"My mom is really messing with it," he says.

I nod because I get the mom thing. I almost tell him about

how embarrassing my mom was on Friday night, but decide against it because there's only a certain level of humiliation you can handle in a day and I'm sure my project confession (plus my failed attempts at funny) will get me there. Instead I just say, "I know, moms are the worst. Always messing with projects and stuff."

Peter stops and considers me a second. "I thought you said your mom *wanted* you to do the paper towel experiment."

Oh, wait. That's right. I said that last time we talked. I blamed it on my mom and how she wanted me to do it so she knew which brand to buy at the store. Then he suggested I could do that experiment for my mom but do an actual cool one for the science fair. I acted like my mom would never go for it.

"She does want me to do it. It's just that she's all interested in the results and she keeps nagging me for them. You know, for her"—and suddenly every possible reason of paper towel usage escapes me—"cooking and stuff."

Peter tilts his head and frowns but doesn't say anything. He studies me like *I'm* the science project.

"But anyways, whatever." I shrug, trying to shake off the attention. "How is your mom messing with the uh. . . . um, your project?"

Still watching me, he raises an eyebrow. "For the reasons you might think she's messing with it."

It's like he's got heated vision. My entire body feels like it's sitting inside my mom's Crockpot.

My charade of calm is dissolving. I lean back in my chair and try to embody a picture of Laid-Back Person. It doesn't work. I glance at Fred and mimic his laid-back posture. It's hard to balance.

Peter asks, "So what are those reasons exactly?"

I'm about to fall out of my chair. I'm so uncomfortable. I sit up. I can't be like Fred even in sitting position. *Come on, be better. Go big.* "Because of all the . . . smells. And stuff."

"The smells!" Peter laughs out loud and a couple of people glance at us. I feel a surge of pride for causing his outburst. It's pushed away by irritation because I didn't mean to be funny right then.

"Smells," Peter says again and holds his pencil over the paper. "This is really interesting. I've never thought about that. I need to write this down. Please, tell about some of the smells."

I could stop now. I *should* stop now.

But I don't because he's laughing at me—and not in the good way. He thinks he's better than me. I refuse to back down.

He said flight . . . so birds. They fly. What else do I know about them?

"Well, there's the poop," I say.

Peter's eyes get so big I think they're going to pop off his head. Then, suddenly, he lets out this enormous, shockingly loud, guffaw-type thing. More follow, and I can't tell if he's laughing or having a seizure.

Everybody in the class is now fully watching us.

I want to run away. But I can't. Because I'm frozen. Peter is laughing so hard he's holding his stomach. Little pig-sound snorts escape from his mouth.

Then there's this little vibrating noise coming out of my throat, and I can't tell if I'm about to laugh or freak out.

Peter snorts again, and I feel my face crinkle.

It's contagious. Now I'm laughing too. Cracking up. Apparently I'm having a mental breakdown. I can barely breathe. I can barely see Ms. Harding as she walks over to us.

I try to breathe deep and calm down. Right when I think I'm going to be okay and will be able to pull out of this tailspin, Peter says, "There's *poop*," and we both lose it again.

Then Ms. Harding is standing there, her million-braceleted hands on her hips. "I've always thought science was amusing as well."

We both stop laughing and sit up really fast, but Peter can't control it and his shoulders are shaking again and he's gone, all snorts and false stops. Idiot. Why won't he shut up?

Our teacher leans down and I know we are about to get in so much trouble, but she just whispers, "You are disturbing the other groups. Please go out into the hall."

Immediately my face burns and I grab my notebook and stand to do the walk of shame, but Peter doesn't seem worried at all. He barely manages to compose himself as we step out of the classroom.

My giddy is all gone. I sit next to the door and suddenly I want to be back inside. I don't want to be out here with Peter. Wild-haired, laughing-at-me, poop-is-funny Peter.

Peter puts his back to the wall and uses it to slide down into a sitting position beside me. He makes this little "hmmmm" sound as he covers his face with his hands. He slaps himself on the face. "Okay." *Slap, slap.* "I'll be okay in just a minute." *Slap.*

He cracks up again.

"I'm almost done. Sorry . . . *There's poop.*"

And then I have to wait a good ten seconds before he repeats the slapping, breathing, sputtering process all over again.

"I don't know what was so funny," I say.

"You were laughing too," Peter says rubbing his eyes.

"Because *you* were."

"Yeah. Because it was *hilarious.*"

I wait for him to be normal again. It takes another two cycles, but he finally manages to stop losing it.

"So," he says, leaning back against the wall. He's still breaking out into spontaneous smiles. "You think my mom doesn't like my experiment because of the poop?"

Admit guilt or pretend to be an idiot? I don't like either option, so I level my eyes at him and don't answer, hoping I can make him talk instead.

It works, but unfortunately not to my advantage.

"Whose poop am I supposedly working with?"

I still don't answer.

"You really don't know what I'm working on, do you?"

"Yes, I do."

"Really?" He sits up straight. He's getting serious now. He's still smiling, but his laugh is gone. "Tell me about my project. In your own words."

I roll my eyes to let him know how stupid I think this is, but he just sits there. Watching me. Waiting.

"Animals. Birds," I say and he doesn't tell me I'm wrong. I start feeling a little cocky. Like maybe I do understand and it's just that stupid of a project. "Flying. Flight. See. I was *listening*."

"And what about the poop? Where does that come into play?"

"That's why your mom doesn't like it. Because that's what birds do."

He nods. "I stand corrected. It's not that you don't understand. It's just that you don't have a single freaking clue about anything I've ever said."

"Yes, I—" I start, but I stop when I see the way he's sitting there all patient and understanding with his face sympathetic. Anger floods my brain and rushes to my lips. Before I can stop it, I say, "No. It's your project. It's . . . *dumb*. And you know what else is dumb? You with taking those pictures."

He's definitely not laughing now. He sits up straighter and pushes up his glasses.

"You know what . . . ?" I'm just about to really let loose and tell him just exactly how stupid it all is, that people are laughing at him, but his expression stops me. What am I saying? What did I say? I need to take it all back.

Before I can speak, Peter says, "Yeah, well. It probably is. But maybe I don't care." His eyes are on the floor. He reaches out to trace an edge of one of those flat, shiny tiles.

I've crossed a line. I need to apologize. But I can't make myself. I don't trust myself to get the words right.

We both sit there, silent and awkward. All the venom has drained out and left me defeated. Ashamed. I am done.

I'm so *done*.

And mad and upset and embarrassed and stupid and lonely and not funny and just so, so done.

So I stand up. And I leave him there.

Peter says my name once, but I don't stop walking. It takes every bit of self-control I have, but I keep my promise to my mom and don't leave the school.

I push through the swinging door of the boys' bathroom, go to the biggest stall, and sit, fully clothed, on the toilet and stare at the closed door. I focus my energy on hating everything about this stupid place (see Figure 13).

Figure 13. List of things I hate

I go straight to lunch when the bell rings. I don't want to go back to get my stuff in Ms. Harding's class because:

1. I don't want to see Peter; and

2. I just don't even care anymore.

I grab my lunch from my locker, and since today is awful, my locker decides to break and won't shut. I slam it, using every ounce of anger. It rebels and flings open. Now I hate my locker too. I grab my stuff and leave it wide open.

In the cafeteria, I go to Fred's table and throw my notebook in my chair and sit on it. Jenna's already there and I sneak a peek at her to see if she has any reaction to me. She doesn't.

Well, good.

I didn't want to deal with her anyway.

Justin is at the table. I'm hoping he's cooled down a little since second period and he realizes I didn't mean to make him lose. He isn't even all the way in his seat before he says, "What's with you and that notebook, dude? You carry it around everywhere, and now you're, like, trying to hatch it."

So, good. At least I know he still hates me.

I shrug and busy myself opening my lunch bag to show him that *I* can let things roll off without overreacting (the way he should have after a dumb basketball game). I lean over my fruit cup, giving it my full attention. I pull open the lid and the juice sloshes all over the table—because of course it would.

"Is it your diary or something?" Justin says as Riley sits down. They both watch me like I'm a TV.

"Leave him alone, Justin. He doesn't want to talk about it," Jenna says.

He makes a face at her. Jenna glares at him. I ignore them both by concentrating really hard on unwrapping my sandwich.

"Is anybody done with their science project yet?" Jenna asks suddenly.

The question is so forced, I know she's trying to help me, but why? Does she feel sorry for me? Or does it mean she read my notebook? Or does she think I can't hang?

Well, guess what, Jenna? I can.

"I finished mine this weekend," Jenna continues. "I think it's pretty good."

Justin rolls his eyes. "Sometimes when you tell the truth," he says, using air quotes as he says "truth," "it just sounds like bragging."

Jenna shrugs. "So."

"I'm using the same one as last year," Fred says, "So I'm done. And it's awesome."

"Ross, I hope you're almost finished," Justin says. "It will give you more time to write in your diary."

"I do *not* have a diary," I say before Jenna can defend me.

"Don't feel bad about it, Ross," Justin says, smirking. "My baby sister has one too and—"

"He said he doesn't have a diary," Jenna snaps.

Oh great, she knows. She did read it and she's going to out me right here and now. My fists are clenching. My face feels hot.

But before she can sell me out, something hits my foot. I'm so tense, I jump and almost fall out of my chair. "You left your backpack." It's Peter. Like a confused, rabid rabbit, my anger hops from Justin and onto Peter.

"Thanks," I say, hoping my tone conveys what I really mean: Go *away*.

"I told Ms. Harding you felt sick and went to the bathroom."

"Awesome," I say through clenched teeth. Now everybody's probably picturing me in the bathroom. Even *I'm* picturing me in the bathroom.

Go *away, Peter*, I think to him. Out loud, I say, "Thanks

again." I raise my eyebrows and nod to try to communicate: *We're done now.*

"Right," Peter says standing there, awkwardly shifting his weight from one foot to the other. Why won't he just leave?

His hand clenches tighter on his lunch bag. For the first time since I've met him, he seems uncomfortable. Even his hair is limp.

"And we should probably figure out some time to meet. For the project. I don't want to get a bad grade just because you—"

"Okay," I cut him off before he says anything incriminating.

Peter stands up straighter. He's so stiff, I bet I could poke him with one finger in the shoulder and knock him down. He glances up and then down again. He seems as aware as I am that everybody in a two-table radius is staring at him. He clears his throat. "We could—"

"We'll meet after school. In the front after the last bell." I'm forced to save us both. It's like somebody in a sinking ship rescuing a guy from drowning in the ocean. "We can talk then."

He smiles for a fraction of a second and nods. Then, finally, he's gone.

"I can't believe you got him as your partner," Justin says when he leaves. "He's so weird."

"Yup," I say, thankful we've got some reason to agree, something in common so we can be friends again. "Totally lost out on that one."

Jenna frowns. "He's smart, too. And a good guy." But she doesn't deny the weird.

She really does have to weigh in on everything. Thank goodness she's here to point out all that I'm doing wrong. "Sorry. I didn't realize he was your boyfriend."

Jenna glares at me. "I'm just pointing out that y'all were having fun earlier in class. Now you're being mean. And he doesn't deserve that. *He's* nice."

"Yeah," Justin says, "he's a nice guy obsessed with video games and taking pictures, who apparently doesn't own a mirror."

"A *nice guy*," Jenna repeats. She's focuses on me with laser eyes. "Who doesn't change himself so people will like him."

I glare back at her, but I can't hold it and look away first.

Justin stuffs three Doritos in his mouth. "Maybe he should. Is that what you write about in your diary, Ross?" he asks. "Dear Diary, my partner is a weirdo."

"He doesn't write about that!" Jenna yells. "It's not a diary."

She's totally about to sell me out. I have to stop her. I join Justin's bit. "Dear Diary," I make my voice all nasally. "I'm afraid my partner's hair is going to poke my eye and blind me."

Jenna pushes her chair back, the feet scraping the floor angrily. She crumples up her lunch bag and stomps off.

"Dear Diary." Justin pretends to write in an imagery notebook. "My partner is a weirdo and my secret crush hates me."

I roll my eyes and laugh like I think it's funny. (Note for my research: When it's mean, it's not.)

WHEN I SPOT Peter after school, he's already striding toward me like a normal-person walk would waste his time. Unfortunately, Peter's efficiency means I can't pretend I don't see him like I'd planned to do.

"Where do you want to go?" he says when he gets to me. "We could go to my house or the library?"

"Home," I say. I nod to the line of buses idling in the pick-up area. "I forgot I have to catch a bus." I don't mention that Pops's house is close enough that I could walk instead.

"You said we could meet now," he borderline-yells. "We're already behind! This project is a big deal."

"I know, but . . ." I hold my hand out toward the buses to show him they're already closing the doors. "I meant maybe we could meet up for, like, a second and make a plan about when we could meet for longer."

Peter looks at me like I've offered him pre-chewed gum. "They make phones for that, you know," he says, poking me in the chest. "They also make brains for thinking and ears for listening, but you don't know how to use any of those." He tips his head back and throws up his hands. "I always get partnered with the idiots."

"Whatever." I decide not to offer to come early before school tomorrow, since he said that. As soon as Pops gets better we'll be gone. None of this will even matter. "I've gotta go." The buses are inching forward. Some have already left. Mine speeds up like it's about to pull out too. I run so I don't miss it.

"Hey!" I yell as the bus line creeps forward. "Hey!" Everybody's probably looking at me, but I don't care. I don't want to stay here. And I definitely don't want to hang out with Weird Peter. "Let me in!" I bang on the side, the bus stops, and the doors squeak and barely open—it's the first decent thing to happen to me today.

"Don't hit my bus," the driver says.

"Sorry," I say to the white-haired, super-skinny guy. A guy I don't recognize.

"Whatdoyawant?" he asks. Behind us somebody honks.

"I need to go home."

The doors are only cracked halfway so I put my hands flat against the glass and push to open them more.

He lets me climb on, but he shakes his head. "You don't ride this bus."

"Yes, I do," I say, but it comes out weak and needy, like I'm begging. I *am* begging. Because I know everybody's watching me now. I'm sure Peter has a front row seat and he's totally enjoying this.

There's another honk from behind, but Mr. White Hair ignores it.

"Where you going?" So I tell him Pops's address (Mom made me memorize it the day I got lost) and he shakes his head. "This bus don't go there. Sorry, bud, I'd help you, but I gotta get these guys home."

I nod and don't argue. There's no reason to. I step off the stairs. The doors close and the bus drives away. All I can do is stand there and watch.

Only the honking bus is left. It's not mine either.

I watch Mr. Honks-a-Lot pull out of the school drive.

It's quiet behind me. I can't make myself turn around. I could walk to Pops's house, except I've lost the motivation to move at all. I'm just going to stand here until tomorrow. Or maybe tomorrow's tomorrow. I give up on today, because it is literally the worst day I've ever had (see Figure 14).

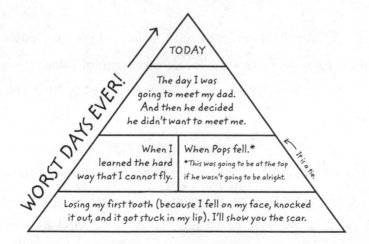

Figure 14. Worst days ever

"I'm not going to lie to you," Peter says as he walks up next to me, "that was hard to watch."

"Shut up," I say, and he does.

Peter is right. He did get paired with an idiot.

He stands there with me and we watch the last bus become a little yellow dot and then totally disappear from sight.

Then he takes out his phone. He's got to be joking.

"Please. Don't take my picture right now."

He scrunches his face and says, "I'm not. I'm telling my mom we're going to the house."

When he clicks the phone off, he says, "Come on, let's go."

Since I've failed at BIG and at being Me, But Better, I've got nothing left to lose. So I listen.

WE'RE QUIET ON the walk to his house. I don't have anything to say. Actually, that's a lie. I don't have anything I *want* to say.

"We're here," Peter says after an extremely long eleven minutes.

His home looks a lot Pops's—the sort of thing a kindergartener would draw if they were told to draw a house. It has reddish brick, one story, big windows, and a square and perfect yard. The one exception is the flag hung in one of the windows: a white rectangle outlined with red and a blue star in the middle.

"Mom's still at work." We put our backpacks on the floor next to three pairs of identical, perfectly aligned black boots. The inside of the house is not like my grandpa's. It's cleaner—both the way it looks and the way it smells. Instead of a blanket-covered sofa and dining room chairs with TV trays in front, there's a big, gray, L-shaped couch with hard edges. Instead of a bunch of (mostly crooked) pictures hung on a butter-colored background, there's empty white walls. The only picture is above the mantel. It's huge and nice and the professional kind that is taken by people that have families they want to show off. It has a man, a woman, and a kid that looks a lot Peter except with normal hair.

"So," Peter says, "you want something to eat?"

I want to say no, but I'm starving, so I tell him I do. We go into his kitchen and I stand there all super aware of the angles of my elbows and how straight I'm standing as he gets out an apple, cuts in into slices, and puts it in the middle of the table. He grabs a bag of cheese cubes from the fridge. "Help yourself," he says, handing me a plate and sitting down.

I follow his lead and crunch into an apple. Neither of us speak. I'm painfully aware of every bite. Sitting directly across from Peter and eating in silence is even more uncomfortable than our walk here.

After we're both squirming from the silence, Peter asks, "Are you finally ready to listen?"

"Yeah." I don't really have another choice.

"Okay," he says. I really *am* about to listen, to ignore all the weird of my partner, but then he pulls out his phone and holds it out so we're both in the frame. He snaps a picture.

"So my project—"

"Why do you do that?"

"Do what?"

"The picture thing. You don't even ask first."

"Oh. Sorry." He looks confused like he doesn't, or can't, understand why I wouldn't like it. "You don't want your picture taken?"

"No!" I answer.

His lips fall into a straight line. He nods. "I'm sorry. I didn't realize . . . I won't do it again."

He shoots up from his chair so fast his legs hit the table and it shakes. I think he's mad and he's going to storm out, but he just takes our plates to the sink and sits down again.

Suddenly it's not awkward anymore. Maybe because I remember I don't even care what Peter thinks. "So let's go. Tell me about your project so I can go home."

His eyes are on the table like he's studying it. He rubs an invisible smudge with his thumb. "I send them to my dad. The pictures. That's why I take them."

His unsure expression calms me down. I take a deep breath. "Um, can I be honest?"

"Why stop now?"

"You didn't make it less weird."

He laughs. I do too. It feels good. Maybe because it's the first time I've really and honestly laughed in a loooooooooong time.

"He's gone. Deployed. My dad. I e-mail pictures so he doesn't miss our life. Mom and mine and his. We got a new kid at school, so I took your picture. You were my partner, so I took it again. It just feels like the e-mails, the phone calls, they aren't enough. I want him to see it all—so he gets the whole story. So he remembers he's got to come back to us."

"Oh," is all I can say. If Mom left, it'd be awful. And I if thought the pictures would be better, I'd do it too. No matter what anybody thought.

"Okay." I nod. "I sort of get it now. You should just ask first."

"Okay."

That quick, Peter makes so much more sense to me. I just didn't get I was missing pieces. There must be more I'm not getting. "So what about your hair?"

"What about it?"

"Is that because of your dad too? Like you won't cut it until he comes back? Is there a reason you let it go all crazy?"

"Yeah, there's a reason." He smirks and pats his head. "It's because it is awesome."

I roll my eyes. Maybe I don't have to understand him completely.

"We'll have to agree to disagree on that," I say.

He laughs. "Agreed. Okay. Are you finally ready to give me feedback on my project?"

"Yeah, just one thing first."

"Uh," he tips his head back. "You are one of the worst listeners, you know that?"

I nod. "I do. I just wanted to tell you I'm sorry." I mean it as both self-description and apology. "I didn't get you before. I guess I needed the Full Peter Experience to appreciate it."

He shrugs. "You're still ahead of the game then. Most people never realize my awesomeness. . . . But you do bring up a good point."

"You need a buzz cut?"

"Never!" He pats his hair protectively. "Some things are better understood through actual experience."

I AM PART of Peter's project. A test subject.

I'm sitting on the couch in Peter's living room all hooked up to a computer. I've got a clip with a red light on my fingers, a blood pressure cuff thing on my arm, and five electrodes stuck to my chest. Peter is double-checking that they're all in the right place; he studies a paper, studies me, and then checks the paper again. His mom, Mrs. Anderson, is there too. She got all this equipment from the doctor's office where she works, and she's making sure he's doing it all right, and, I'm sure, that we don't break it.

I'm not totally sure what's about to happen. I know just enough to be afraid. Peter said his experiment is supposed to test my response to stress. When you're scared, he said, your body automatically takes over with one of two possible outcomes: Fight or Flight. In the first, you stay and deal with whatever is bugging you. In the second, you run away (see Figure 15).

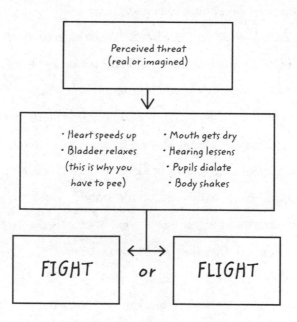

Figure 15. Fight or flight response to fear

We had to wait for Peter's mom to get home since we're using a bunch of expensive equipment from her office. Plus, she wanted to call my mom and make sure it was absolutely, positively, one hundred percent okay that Peter tested me for his experiment.

Even after Mom and I both said it was okay, like, a thousand and three times, Mrs. Anderson is still trying to talk me out of it. "You can't unsee or unlearn things. Once they are in, they're in." She points a finger to her head to show me where exactly they'd be "in."

"Mom," Peter says as he finishes checking to make sure everything is on right, "it's going to be okay."

Mrs. Anderson shakes her head. As she's making sure Peter's hooking me up correctly, she says, "I still remember my first scary movie. I was traumatized. I had nightmares. Barely slept for weeks."

"I know, Mom," Peter says, patting her on the shoulder as he finishes up. "Everyone here knows. Because you already told us. A million times." She frowns at Peter and he gives her a double thumbs-up. "But we really enjoyed the story!"

Mrs. Anderson turns to me. "If you want to stop at any time—"

"I promise to let you know," I finish for her.

She nods. "You're a good boy."

Her compliment makes me smile. Too bad I'm lying. I'm pretty nervous actually.

"You ready?" Peter asks.

"Yup," I say.

"You worried?"

"Nope."

Peter raises an eyebrow. "You remember I have a pulse monitor hooked up to you, right?" He points to the thing clipped to the end of my finger. "I seriously doubt your normal rate is around a hundred or you've got problems."

"Oh, I've definitely got problems."

Peter laughs. "Don't worry. I'll still be able to tell when you're *really* freaked out. It'll go up even more when you are about to pee your pants."

"Awesome. Thanks," I say.

Peter shrugs. "It's what friends do."

I hope he doesn't notice my heart beating harder when he calls me a friend.

Peter pretends to pop his knuckles and then he turns on the TV. "And now, it's about to get interesting. Mom, you ready?"

His mom sits down in front of the computer and Peter tells me to watch the movie. He picks up a clipboard and pen, checks the computer screen, and immediately starts writing stuff. "Okay, Ross, all you have to do is sit back and enjoy."

On the TV there's a girl. She's running fast—not stopping even though she's breathing hard. She keeps looking back over her shoulder. I can't see anything behind her yet, but the creepy music makes me think something bad is definitely coming. My heart beats harder as I watch her.

"Hey, Peter," I lean over and whisper loudly, my eyes still on the screen.

"Yeah?"

"She's using the flight response."

He laughs.

And BOOM! On the movie, a guy in a white mask and a black robe JUMPS out next to the girl.

I flinch (and *maybe* scream a little). I glance at Peter, expecting him to make some comment about my scaredy-cat reaction, but he doesn't.

"Keep watching the TV."

I hold my breath as I watch both characters, the girl and the mask-wearing-scary-person, run across the screen. The guy's chasing her, getting closer and closer . . . he's almost got the girl. He reaches out. . . . I clench my fists, now super sure that Peter's watching me, and all the stuff hooked up to me is telling him that I'm freaking out.

The girl gets away. Then I can breathe.

She's running faster now, not paying attention to what's in front of her. She's going, going, going. The movie shows her feet running, crunching the grass. Then it is back to a full view of her. She's pushing through the trees, checking behind her—*stop looking back, dummy!*—and then, and then—she runs smack into him. She falls down. He reaches for her, and . . . I can't watch. I duck my head and shut my eyes.

No, wait. I didn't mean to do that.

I open my eyes immediately. The TV is blank. Peter puts down the remote. "Huh," he says as he writes something on the clipboard.

I stand up, trying to erase the last scene from my brain. "What do you mean, 'huh?'"

He shrugs. "I'm surprised by your reaction, that's all."

"My reaction? Why? What'd I do?" I start to remove the pulse reader, and he stops me.

"Ahh, nothing. Don't worry about it. But you know what? I've gotta talk to my mom about something."

He sets down the clipboard on the edge of the computer desk. I can see writing, but no way I can read it.

"Hey, Mom. Will you come here for a minute, please?"

Mrs. Anderson glances at me like she wants to ask if I'm okay, but she doesn't say anything. She stands up and follows Peter to the hall.

What is he talking to her about? And why did he say, "*huh?*"

I hold my breath and stay super still and try to hear them talking.

I can't.

But the clipboard is on the edge of the table and if I stand up and lean over . . . just a little . . . maybe I can read it.

I double-check the doorway to make sure nobody's coming, and stand up. I keep my left foot planted and step with my right foot and *lean* forward as far as I can without messing up the wires.

I still can't read it. At first I think it's because I'm not close enough, but I lean a little more and realize there is nothing much to read. There's just wavy lines, rows and rows of them. Like the kind little kids make when they think they're writing words. But in the middle of the paper they stop and in big block letters, it says, "BOO."

What in the—

Suddenly a guy with a white mask and a black robe lunges from around the corner.

I definitely scream this time as I step backwards and trip over my own feet and the wires and land on my butt.

My brain tells me I'm toast, but the maniac doesn't come toward me. Instead, he reaches up and pulls off his mask.

As I tell my heart to stay *inside* my body, Peter, mask in hand, is laughing but he still manages to say, "I'm really sorry." *Hahahaha.* "You looked so scared." *Hahahaha.* "Are you okay?"

Words are not my friends yet. My mouth is too dry to work.

Peter holds his hand out to me. "Thanks, man. You're a good sport."

I let him pull me up as I try to stop breathing like I've just run a mile. Underwater.

In a second, I might be mad at him for laughing at me, but currently I'm just so glad it was him in a mask and not the movie psycho.

I bend down and put my hands on my knees for a few seconds to make it easier to breathe. "If I had listened the first time you told me, would I've known that was going to happen?"

Peter is nice enough to look sorry for me as he nods. Then, like he's trying to make me feel better, he says, "Do you want to guess which response you had?"

"Flight?" I say.

He nods. "You definitely had flight."

"Yes," I agree. "I flew . . . like a penguin. Although . . ." I turn around and look down.

"What's wrong?" he asks.

Peter is looking at the floor too, trying to see what I'm worried about.

I smile, "Just making sure. That was pretty intense—and I seem to remember something about poop."

We both crack up.

MOM PICKS ME up from Peter's house and tells me she's got something exciting to show me. My expectations are low, considering she uses the same build-up any time she gets a new bassoon (and never for the dog or cat or even guinea pig I've always wanted).

When we get home, the first thing I notice is that the boxes are cleared out of the entryway, which is actually a little annoying because now we have to find a new place for my backpack and stuff, and I think Mom's surprise is that she's cleaned up. But then I notice the cane leaning against the wall and then an edge of the walker poking from around the corner. It's like gigantic metal bread crumbs leading to the thing Mom wanted to show me: Pops is home.

He's sitting on the couch with a bunch of pillows surrounding him. When he sees me seeing him, he sits up straighter and his eyes get clearer. "Hey, kid," he says.

He looks so much better. "Pops!" I give him a huge hug. Mom reminds me I need to be careful.

"Daddy, this is Ross."

He sighs and shakes his head. "I know that." He pats the middle of the cushion of the couch and says, "Now sit here, kid. I saved the best seat just for you."

I sit and don't even point out the middle of the couch is actually the worst seat. I'm just glad he's better. Plus, the timing is perfect. We'll definitely be gone before the science fair now. This day has totally turned around. The world is brighter. It's like when one of the bulbs goes out in your bedroom. At first you get used to the dimness, then you change it and almost need sunglasses inside.

Mom sits down too and we start watching a TV show together. Pops makes it a solid few minutes before his head tips back and he's breathing hard and steady, warming up for a full-fledged snore.

We let him sleep and go to the kitchen to eat dinner. Mom serves chicken and I scoop rice and we laugh when Pops's pre-snore morphs into the real thing.

She asks me if I had fun at Peter's. I'm about to tell her I went over for a school project and it wasn't a going-to-a-friend's-house-for-fun sort of thing, but that description seems wrong too. Because it *was* fun. I might even actually miss Peter after we leave. We can e-mail though.

After we did Peter's science project, it was like his mom felt bad, so she made up these cinnamon apple things and let us play video games and then we watched the video (he'd secretly recorded) of me sneaking up to read the clipboard and then falling on my rear over and over and over because we both thought it was so hilarious. I mean, maybe I wasn't a huge fan the first time I saw it, but that lasted for about thirty-three seconds until I realized I was basically the star of the funniest thing I'd ever seen.

I'm still cracking up as I tell Mom about it now and she's laughing too and it's like this moment of "aha" where everything feels on the warm side of perfect.

And then Pops lets out the loudest snore yet.

Mom and I lose it—like tears in our eyes and trouble breathing. We're probably the reason Pops wakes up and calls Mom back to the living room.

It's while she's going that two things pop into my head. Those are: 1. We were so busy at Peter's that I never told him the truth about my project; and 2. Now Pops is home, so I don't have to!

My leg starts shaking when I also realize 3. I've been so busy with attempting funny and going big that I've completely abandoned my Exit-lence planning.

When Mom comes back in and sits down, I ask what I need to know. "So how long does Pops need us here? When do we leave?"

The lip biting starts hard and fast. "Remember, we talked about his. How he's not quite ready to be on his own."

"Well, yeah," I say to calm her down. This is a good thing actually. Gives me time to plan. "That makes sense. It's not like we need to go tomorrow."

"Really?" Mom says. "I thought you'd be ready to leave by now."

I've got another two weeks until the science project is due.

I shake my head. "Nah. I can definitely last another week. Almost two if I had to."

Mom threads her fingers together and rests her elbows on the table. "Ross, he's a lot better, but I think it's going to be a little longer than that."

"Okay. Like, three weeks?" It's definitely pushing it, but maybe I could make that work. I could pretend I'm not done and get an extension. The presentation could be part of the Exit-lence. I've never started with a captive audience before. The thought makes me both giddy and nervous. It'd be a lot of pressure to perform in the spotlight like that.

"The doctor said it'll take at least two months."

Like he wants to prove a point, Pops's snore morphs to a gurgle and then a full-on choke. Mom stands and hurries to the living room.

I don't want to go, but when he doesn't stop coughing, I check on him too.

His face is red and he looks like he's struggling, but he holds up a finger to tell us to wait.

Finally he stops. To Mom he croaks, "Tissue." To me he says, "Hey, kid." Since Mom left to get Pops what he wanted, she's not here to correct him, and I don't know if I'm supposed to, so I just say, "Hey, adult." He chuckles and chokes again.

Mom runs back. He takes the tissue from her and, mid-choking, calmly folds it into a square and wipes at his mouth. His hands shake. He's so old and fragile. It sort of freaks me out.

"You gonna sit down with me again?" His voice is hoarse.

I sit and he leans over and pats me on the knee. "Kid, I don't know what I'd do without you here."

"Well, I guess you won't have to for a while." I can't make myself look at him. I *know* it's not fair to be mad at him—but it's also not fair we have to stay.

"That's so good to hear." He clears his throat and adjusts the pillows to sit up straighter. He seems lighter somehow. I, on the other hand, feel like I'm wearing an anchor as a necklace.

But I guess between the two of us, it makes more sense for me to take on the extra weight.

RECORD THE RESULTS/ ORGANIZE YOUR DATA

Include tables, charts, and graphs.

DESPITE ALL MY efforts, this is what I know:

I am Me, and definitely Not Better (maybe even worse).

I will have to turn in (and present) a science fair project.

I have totally and completely failed at both going BIG and in the science of funny.

I need a new project.

My weekend starts with searching the Internet for non-humiliating science fair projects.

My plan was to find one on Saturday and do tons of brainstorming and researching Sunday. Then Monday I'd get the okay I needed from Ms. Harding and share my real project with Peter. After that I'd have a week to test and one week to write it up and get ready for the presentation.

But yesterday morning I tried Googling and Mom kept coming in and bugging me, so I decided to hang out with her for a while instead. After lunch, I tried again, but I kept falling asleep as I read through the websites, so I decided to watch TV with Pops for a while and push the project decision back a day.

Now that it's Sunday, I'm back in front of my computer. The science project page is open; Mom hasn't bugged me once, but I still can't concentrate.

I keep imagining standing up in front of the class to present and failing miserably. Peter's project keeps popping into my head. Specifically, the *video* from Peter's project. The video of me.

Which shows my reaction to Peter's project: I ran away.

I *ran* from Peter in the mask.

I mean, I didn't know it was Peter at the time. My brain didn't really reason. I just saw a guy coming at me, the same guy I'd seen already come at somebody else, and I ran.

I don't *really* even know if the thing got that girl or not because when he reached for her, I closed my eyes.

Which, really, is just another way of running.

So, my conclusion: I'm a flight-er.

And sure, lots of people are going to run if they think a bad guy's going to get them. That's the smart thing to do in that specific scenario. But the thing is, I didn't just do it at Peter's house.

I did it the first day I came to this school.

I did it when Peter and I got sent out into the hall.

I did it when I was supposed to meet Peter after school.

Every time I had a problem, running away was my response (see Figure 16).

Even my Exit-lence was just a spectacular way to run.

And the whole time we've been here, it's continued. No wonder I've failed. It is impossible to run from myself.

FIGHT	FLIGHT
ECHO ... ECHO ... ECHO ... ECHO ...	• When I tripped over Shana's bag (even though I played it off) • First day of school • Lying about my project • Dealing with Jenna • Peter's project • Still not telling Peter about my project • Trying to change my project because I'm not funny

Figure 16. Examples of when I've used the fight or flight response

I am a flight-er.

But I don't want to be.

From: nomadman@nma.com

To: herecomeztreble@nma.com

Subject: Here's hoping the truth will set me free.

I've haven't been honest with you in a long time. I actually don't want to be honest with you now, but I've got to start somewhere and you are the safest. I think. I hope.

I was a little mad at you. Sometimes I still am (even though I KNOW I shouldn't be). I know I say it like I'm kidding, but I'm not.

I'm really sorry.

It's not your fault at all. It's all mine. It just seemed like everything was going great for you and plus I missed you. I wanted to blame you for that. I'm still jealous actually. Things just work out for you. I, on the other hand, mess up everything I touch.

More truth: I can't be Me, But Better. Sometime I barely want to be Me. But I'm trying to change that.

I get it if you want to cancel our summer plans. Sometimes I have a hard time being around me too.

Ross

"PETER," I CALL out when I see him walk into school Monday morning.

Even though there's only a few minutes until the bell and we're both about to be late, he stops and waits for me. "Hey. Have an okay weekend? My mom was terrified you were going to have nightmares because of my project."

It was actually a terrible weekend because of his project—but not because of nightmares.

It's because I was making a plan to stop flight-ing and start fight-ing.

That is why I need to talk to Peter right now.

"I wanted to tell you about my project." I tap the notebook that I'm carrying. "I'll make it quick."

"Big happenings in the paper towel world or something?" I walk down the hallway with him.

"So my project isn't really about paper towels."

"Thank goodness," Peter says, stopping in front of his locker and opening it. "That one is horrible." He pulls out a book, shoves his bag in, and shuts the door. "So what is it really?"

I force myself to tell him the truth, even though there is a high probability he's going to think my real project is even lamer than my fake one. And that I have to admit I've lied. And failed. "My project is," I lean in so only he can hear, "how to be funny."

He frowns. "What?"

My face burns but I keep going. "How to be funny. Like figuring out the things that make people laugh and the things that don't."

He raises his eyebrows and nods. "Okay. Cool."

"That's it? Just 'cool.'"

"I figure you'll tell me the rest of it during science. Like how you're actually testing it and stuff. You do have a plan, right?"

"Yeah . . . well, sort of. I did. Turns out, I'm no comedian."

"Sure you are. You've made me laugh."

"Never on purpose."

"Does that matter?" He glances at his watch again. "I gotta go. We'll talk in science. We can figure it out then."

FIRST RESULT OF being a fight-er: relief.

Seriously.

Why didn't I tell Peter so much sooner?

We're out in the hall again. Ms. Harding sent us here when we wouldn't stop laughing. I was telling about Peter my notebook of research, explaining the TV shows I watched, and then I read him the jokes I wrote down. He laughed a little at first and then harder and harder. Watching him laugh made me laugh. Then he laughed harder and then I did too and so on until we got kicked out.

"This is genius," Peter says. "You're like Einstein meets Tom Sawyer or something. Next year I'm picking a project where research is watching hilarious TV shows and reading joke books."

"So you really think it's okay?"

He shrugs. "I mean, the way you test it is a little weak. You probably won't win first place or anything, but yeah, it works."

"What about presenting it? You know, now that I've figured out that I'm completely unfunny."

"You're not unfunny. Sometimes you just try too hard. Don't take yourself so seriously and have fun with it."

"How do you have fun presenting a science project?"

"I don't know. I'm going to dress up as the scary movie guy. You could dress up like a clown or something."

"Maybe I should throw a pie in Ms. Harding's face when I do my presentation."

Peter laughs. "And then you could throw one at the principal when you are sitting in his office."

I pretend to write in my notebook. "Peer reviewer says: Pie in the face of principal."

* ° * ° *

LUNCHTIME. I STOP by my still-broken locker to grab my lunch. I make sure I've got my notebook and then go to the cafeteria. I'm no longer the kid trying to be something I'm not. BUT I'm also no longer a flight-er, so I sit at the spot I claimed when I first got here—and then I pull up a chair so Peter can sit at this table too.

Nobody mentions our new tablemate when they sit down, but Justin is especially quiet. A couple of times he stares at me, then at Peter, and I think he's going to say something, but he turns his attention to the cafeteria. Every time it happens, I feel like I've barely escaped.

"Hey, Peter," Jenna says when she sits down. She looks at me but doesn't smile and doesn't say anything. It makes me wish I'd sat somewhere else, but now I'm stuck. Leaving now would be flight-ing.

Fred doesn't seem to notice that our table has grown by one. He leans back in his chair and munches on carrots. Peter asks him about some video game I've never heard of and they start talking. I relax.

Then Riley sits down.

She stares at Peter, who doesn't notice because he's so into whatever he's saying to Fred. I try not to watch Riley watching them, but it's hard to look away. She is so purposeful—carefully unzipping her lunch box and taking out the contents, arranging her sandwich and chips and fruit in a neat line like they are soldiers on a battlefield. She's easily got more room in front of her than anybody else, but still, she sighs when she runs out of room for her drink, "It's crowded over here today."

Her comment is all the encouragement Justin needs. "So, Ross, help me understand. A few days ago you can't stand Peter and now y'all are bff's?"

"He never said he couldn't stand him," Jenna says.

I smile at Jenna. "Thanks."

"I'm not helping you. He just wasn't accurate." She looks at Peter. "He was making fun of you. Mostly your hair."

Everybody around us has gone quiet. I'm about to grab my lunch and tell Peter to follow me to the safety of another table, but a nagging voice in my head says, *You* would *do that, flight-er.*

So I steady myself. Because this is it. *This* is where I change.

I turn to Peter. "That was before I knew you. I'm really sorry."

Peter shrugs and nods like it's okay with him. "I'm cool with it."

But Justin won't let it be that easy. He smirks at us and says, "How sweet."

I stare at Justin. He stares back at me. He looks away first.

Peter's the first one to cut through the silence. "He was just jealous." He pats his hair down; it springs back up. "Most people are. Not everybody can be born like this."

I laugh. Riley rolls her eyes. Jenna smiles, first at nothing, then at me.

Justin doesn't look at Peter or me and he doesn't say anything. He just snatches up his drink, sucks it down in one gulp, and then squeezes it into a ball with his hand. From his expression, I think he's pretending I'm the juice box.

Fred gives a very Fred-like shrug and burps.

Riley starts talking with Jenna. Nobody's paying any more attention to me or Peter except for Justin. Order is restored enough that we can ignore him. Finally Justin stops glaring at me.

It's over. Just like that. *Because I fought back.*

We all eat and talk until the end of lunch. Justin even offers me his chips—although I can't be sure he didn't spit on them first.

I get a warm fuzzy feeling as we all sit there. Like I have real-no-kidding-friends. What if, even when Pops is better, I don't want to leave?

Maybe Trent was wrong all along. I don't have to be Me, But Better. I don't have to be anything special or great—I have to be *here*. I just have to stand up for myself and fight my way in. It seems so easy and obvious when I think about it. You don't have to be a special type of water to join the ocean; you just pour yourself in and it makes a spot for you.

I am exuberant.

Light.

My realization is so profound that . . . that . . . that I've totally let my guard down and when the bell rings and Peter and I get up to walk out it takes a solid four seconds before I remember I left my notebook in my chair (see Figure 17).

SECOND 1 → Euphoric

SECOND 2 → Wait. Am I forgetting something?

SECOND 3 → Why, yes. I am forgetting something rather important

SECOND 4 → You've got to be kidding me.

SECOND 4.21 → Oh shoot!

Figure 17. Time lapse of oh-shoot-ness

"'*How to be funny*,'" I hear—everybody hears—Justin say before I can even turn around. "'By Ross Stevens.'" He's standing on my chair, holding my notebook and flipping to the next page.

"Stop it," I say, frantic.

"'The purpose of this experiment is to understand how to be funny,'" he lowers the notebook and says directly at me, "Spoiler alert. You *failed*."

For a second I freeze. My first thought is to walk away. Straight out of the door and to Pops's house and never return. Mom could homeschool me until we go. She would understand why I need to leave this time.

Justin keeps going, loud enough for everybody to hear. "'Research your problem: I will study TV shows, joke books, and real-life examples.'" He laughs. "He's written about all of us in here."

I take a step back and accidentally run into Peter. He doesn't flinch. He never flinches—even when sometimes he should. He's steady. He's Peter.

"'Real-world example one. Awkwardness. When I was in science . . .'"

Everybody is listening to Justin.

Even Fred. Laid-back Fred. He doesn't do anything. Doesn't get bothered by anything. But he also doesn't stand up for anything.

Justin is still reading. I need to stop him.

"I said stop. *Now*." I take a step forward.

Justin doesn't listen. He steps down from the chair and walks toward me, flips a page, and keeps reading. He's smirking. He is confident.

I am not steady. I am not laid-back. I am not confident.

I am indecision and insecurity and flight-ing. But I don't want to be.

I want to fight.

So I do.

I run forward and hit him full force with my body. *Hard*. We both go down.

The notebook lands on the floor next to us.

I don't know what to do next. It feels like I should wait for invisible dust to settle around us or I should get my notebook or I should hit Justin again. Before I decide, I feel Justin's fist connect with my cheek, then with my eye, then exploding my nose.

Turns out, I'm a terrible fight-er.

I'm so definitely losing.

But there's no turning back now.

I get to my knees. I need to keep trying.

There's a bunch of kids around us, watching and screaming. All the voices run together. I have no idea what they are saying.

I clench my fists and stand up. I charge toward Justin, but somebody bigger, stronger grabs me before I get to him. Justin doesn't have the same hindrance and lands one more hit to my jaw. I can't even cradle my face with my hands because they're pinned behind me.

Now some teacher's got Justin too, and we're both being pushed through the crowd. The P.E. teacher is yelling, telling everybody else to sit down and be quiet or they'll join Justin and me.

I'm pulled down the hall by one of the teachers. My face is dripping blood. Some lands on the floor, some lands on my pants. It's warm. There's a lot of it.

As I'm herded past the front office lady, I catch a glimpse of myself in the window. A teacher I don't know is marching me forward. Already one of my eyes is swollen shut. On the opposite side, my lip is puffy. Blood is running out of both sides of my nose.

In the same window, I see Justin's reflection. He's just behind me. He looks untouched.

It's a blur as they sit us down in the counselor's office. I haven't been here since the day I registered.

She's in front of us, talking to us, asking questions.

I think I answer, but I'm more focused on the throbbing in my head. Somebody hands me two ice packs. I press them on either side of my face.

Calls are made. More questions are answered. Parents appear.

When my mom sees me, a gasp sneaks out and her hands fly to her mouth. The principal says something to her. I can only process one of the words: "suspension."

Mom tenses and nods and her lips pinch into a tight line. She walks over to me.

I stand—really, really wanting to cry and really, really trying not to.

She puts one arm around me and uses her other hand to hold onto my shoulder closest to her.

As Mom leads me out of the school, the bell rings and I can feel everybody's eyes on me.

On my beat-up face.

On the tears that I can't stop.

On my mom guiding me out of the school.

I've failed.

I've failed funny. I've failed fighting. I've failed Mom.

I'm a mess. I look ridiculous. Because I am not a fighter. Because once again I tried to be something I'm not. Because at the end of the day, I'm only Me.

INTERPRET THE DATA AND STATE YOUR CONCLUSION

Was your hypothesis true? Was your big question answered?

I CAN'T TELL how mad Mom is right now. I think it is somewhere on a scale from "very" to "acting like a spider and eating her young." Her facial expression hasn't changed since she successfully masked her horror at my bleeding face. Her voice stayed calm when we got into the car, when she verified I was okay, and when we got home and she told me to go to my room. Sooo calm. It was freaky.

Several minutes after I've sunk onto my bed, she comes in and puts two fresh ice packs and a glass of ice water with a straw on my nightstand. I've been lying there, completely still and staring at the ceiling with my one good eye. As she sits on my bed, puts her hand on my leg and says, "I love you?" I curl onto my side.

"When can we leave?" I ask her when I can speak. I'm sort of serious and sort of joking.

She sniffs and when I turn to look at her, she's wiping at her eyes. "I wanted to leave before we got here." She leans forward and picks up the two ice packs and puts them on my face. "Lie back and hold these on there. It'll keep the swelling down."

I obey. My eyes are closed, but I can still feel her sitting next to me. "What happens now?"

"Well, first of all, you're suspended a week for fighting at school."

"Okay."

Mom sighs and I wonder if she's doing it extra loud since I can't see her. "You know this has been really hard on me too."

"But you said you were fine." My voice is muffled.

"No. I said I loved you."

I pulled the ice packs away so I could look at her. "But that's our code."

She puts her hands over mine and replaces the ice on my face. "And I'm realizing that maybe it shouldn't be. Maybe we should actually talk using more than three words."

"We could increase it to seven."

Mom laughs, but in a sad way. "I know it feels a little too serious and a lot too scary. But I think it's necessary. So let's start with the most pressing issue. Let's talk about exactly why I picked up my son early from school because he was all bloody from fighting."

"'Cause I'm really bad at it," I say.

"No. No sarcasm. I want real answers. How did this happen? Not just today, but since we moved here. How did it get to this point?"

The ice packs make me braver, I think, because I don't have to look at Mom as I talk; I don't change my words based on her reaction. Maybe that's why she wants me to hold them there—so I can't see her.

I tell Mom about the project: my topic, the notebook, the research, about how I wanted to be Me, But Better. Then I tell her about Peter and Justin and Riley, about missing my bus, and about going to Peter's house. She listens to it all, and somewhere in the middle lets me take off the ice packs, and even when I see her bite her lips together, I keep going. She laughs when I tell her the "because there's poop" story. She nods when I tell her about Peter's project and how I didn't like my reaction.

We sit in silence for a bit as Mom takes everything in. Finally, she says, "They offered me a permanent job as a high school music teacher. I haven't taken it yet." She sighs. "It's not winning a symphony spot, and it's the same thing over and over all day long. I have to follow curriculum and rules and can't be as creative or spontaneous as I want to be. I don't know if I'm cut out to teach music." She pauses. "Or at least that is what I tell myself."

I nod so she'll keep going. I'm waiting for the punch line.

"And here you are suspended *again*—"

"Technically it is the first time, since they couldn't enforce it at the other schools," I point out.

"*Technically*, it shouldn't have happened at all," she says in a tone that tells me I should continue to be quiet and listen. "I always thought that when we moved, I was making your experience bigger. Giving you the good parts of my childhood and none of the bad. And, if I'm honest, I thought it proved we—I—was strong because I didn't need help. But I think you are right. I think you are a flight-er. I think you learned it from me. And that isn't what I want for us. We can do better."

I try to sit up, but my jaw throbs so much, I groan and lie back down. Mom holds the ice packs on my face.

Mom closes her eyes and swallows. "So we are staying."

"Until Pops gets better?"

"Nope. Much, much longer than that. That's the scarier thing to do for both of us, but we can do it. I'm going to learn to like my job and read all the e-mails from the overly involved parents. And after you serve your time, you are going to go back to school and do everything remotely in your power to never, ever, ever get in trouble again—the way you promised when we got here. You will keep that promise. And I don't just mean you won't get suspended—I mean like you won't even speak in class without raising your hand."

"Since it hurts to talk, that shouldn't be too hard."

"Good. And since we are talking about things that are painful," she says, her voice changing from serious to momness, "let's also talk about all the things from which you are grounded."

IT'S THURSDAY, FOUR days into my suspension and my grounding from anything remotely entertaining. Peter and his mom are here after school. He wants to practice his final presentation in front of me, since we're both presenting on Monday. Mrs. Anderson is here too. She's sitting on the couch pretending to read a magazine. Mom is still at work; she says she can't take off since she's just officially started. I'm overly pumped to see humans other than Mom and Pops. It's been a very long week. Actually serving suspension really stinks.

"Your mom keeps looking at us," I whisper to Peter after I've caught her staring for the fourth time.

"It's okay," he says as he's setting up his display poster. "She's just a little surprised at what happened. She never pegged you for a fighter. Hey, does this graph make sense to you?" He points to a printout on his board.

"Yes," I say without thinking about it. "She's mad at me for fighting?"

"Nah, she's good with it. My dad is one too. She just didn't know you had it in you," he says, stepping back and making sure his poster doesn't fall. "You ready for this awesomeness?"

"Yeah," I say. "She doesn't hate me?"

Peter sighs loudly. "Next year your report should be 'How to Listen' so you can figure out how to do that."

"Sorry."

"Do you want to know how you can tell if my mom doesn't like you?"

I hesitate. "No. Well, yeah. I guess."

"Mom," he calls across the room, "do you like Ross?"

I close my eyes and wait for the embarrassment to pass. It doesn't.

"Peter! Of course I like Ross! Why would you ask that?" His mom is up now and coming over to us. "Are you okay, sweetie? Peter told me what happened." She reaches out and takes my chin so she can turn my face from side to side and inspect it. "Those bruises look *awful*. That young man really beat you up."

"Geez, Mom," Peter says. "Way to make him feel better."

"Sarcasm, young man. It's not welcome. Or funny."

"Hey, you can use that in your project, Ross." He makes a serious face. "Mom says, 'Sarcasm is not funny.'"

"Timing and audience matter for sure," I say after Mrs. Anderson finishes her assessment of my injuries. "It's the when and the who that makes it funny."

"I'm . . . always . . . funny," Pops says, coming into the room.

He's getting stronger now, but the effort of pushing his walker still makes him breathe hard.

"Ross is a good boy, Peter. You should listen to him." She pats me on my shoulder.

"So you want me to get in a fight and get suspended too? Cool." Peter flashes a thumbs-up sign to his mom. "Video game day tomorrow, Ross?"

"I wouldn't call . . . what Ross did . . . fighting," Pops says as he makes it to the couch and lowers himself onto it. He takes out two bottles of water from the bag attached to his walker—one for Mrs. Anderson and one for himself. He seems to have gotten better a lot faster after Mom told him we were planning on staying here for good (for now).

Mrs. Anderson frowns. "I'm worried I had a part in this. Did Peter's experiment cause you a lot of stress?"

Peter rolls his eyes. "Mom, Justin is a jerk. He deserved it. Ross was just being awesome. Will you please go pretend to read your magazine again?"

She goes back to the other side of the room and as she picks up her magazine, she says, "The when and the who, Peter. And here's a hint—right now, it's *not* your mother."

Mrs. Anderson next to Pops and thanks him for the water. He nods and they start talking.

Peter pulls on his black robe. I want to ask him something

before he starts—a nagging question that I need to know now that Mom and I are staying. I glance around to make sure Pops and Mrs. Anderson aren't listening and then lean in so I don't have to talk too loud. "I have a question for you," I tell Peter, taking his advice to just ask if I want to know something.

"Shoot."

"I'm not a fighter—"

"Ross. That is not a question. That's completely obvious."

He puts on the white mask and it makes me braver, since I don't have to see his face. "I'm not done yet. So, I'm not a fighter. I'm not cool. I'm not confident. Why are we friends?"

He shrugs. "Because we are," Peter says, his voice muffled by the mask.

"But why?"

Peter takes off the mask so I can fully see his eye roll. "I don't know. If you make me say it, we're about to not be."

"I'm sorry, I just—"

"Look. We just are. You don't have to be anything else. And you *are* funny when you don't take yourself seriously. And you may not be all cool and hilarious. But you know how everybody says the kids that are actually secretly feel bad about themselves?"

I nod.

"Those people are lying. Those kids have great self-esteem. Of course they would—they are naturally cool and hilarious."

So what am I? Well-rounded? Funny? A delinquent? A runner? A (failed) fighter?

"You are you," Peter says like he knows what I'm thinking. "And yeah, there's good and bad things about that. But you own up to your mistakes and you fix them. You're, I don't know, real. And want to be better. And do you know who I am?"

I start to think of the good things I want to say about him, but before I can, he says, "I'm the guy that always gets partnered with the idiots. Now can you *please* listen to my project so I can be done?"

EVERYBODY TRIES NOT to stare at me as I walk into school Monday morning, but they aren't very good at it. My face still shows the bruises. At least it's not so swollen anymore.

I have a plan of action for today. My first step: stop at Justin's locker—even if I'd rather hide for the rest of the year. Thankfully, he's there so I don't have to awkwardly stand around and wait for him. I hold out my hand just like Peter did the first time I met him. I underestimated the handshake before. It can mean *nice to meet you* or *it's a deal* or, in this case, *I want to apologize*. "I'm sorry."

He rolls his eyes. "Whatever," he says. He ignores my hand, shuts his locker, and walks away.

Not what I was hoping for, but I tried. I take a deep breath and try to let it go.

I take my huge trifold poster into Ms. Harding's room, drop off my books at my locker, and go to my first period class. After a week of TV game shows with Pops (the company was good, but the shows were not), I'm even glad to see Mr. Longfellow.

By science I'm nervous, which I didn't really expect since I practiced my report approximately one thousand and three times. It was the only good thing about my suspension and grounding.

Peter's presentation is right before mine. He puts up the poster board and steps behind it. We can't see what he's doing.

We know he's about to start, so we wait. And wait. And wait. And right when we're all wondering if he's chickened out of his presentation, he pops out and everybody jumps. He's wearing the black robe and white mask. Ms. Harding immediately tells him that is inappropriate—but I think she's just mad because he scared her. He takes off his mask for his presentation. Just like I told him I would, I snap a picture so he can send it to his dad.

Midway through Peter's speech, he starts a video to show people's reactions when he jumped out at them, but about fifteen seconds into it, Ms. Harding asks him if he's gotten permission from the participants to show their reactions. When he says no, she makes him turn it off. She says both him and his peer reviewer should have caught that detail in the handouts we were given.

Yeah, she's definitely mad that he scared her.

But the rest of his presentation is great. It'll be hard to follow. My nerves are gearing up again, dumping bags full of butterflies in my stomach. When Peter starts his last section and I know I'm on deck, the butterflies start cage fighting, but they all freeze in their half-nelsons when I hear what Peter is saying. It's different from the version he practiced at my house.

"I wanted to study people's reactions to fear. My prediction," he points to the "Hypothesis" section of his poster, "was that people either fought or ran away. But my peer reviewer showed me a third option. His first response was flight and he didn't like it. So he tried out the fight response. And I think it's safe to say that didn't work out so well for him."

He points to me and I make a crazy-wide-eyed-weird face to hide my embarrassment. At least my bruises disguise my redness. For a second, I think Peter's mad about everything and he's getting back at me, but he continues. "He's ditching that one too. So he changed my understanding. Because of him, my conclusion is there are three responses when you are afraid. There's *fight*, there's *flight*, or for the really brave, there is *showing up*—even if you know you're going to get the stuffing beat out of you."

And then, because he's Peter, he bows.

Ms. Harding starts clapping and everybody else joins her. It takes me a minute to recover before I can stand up.

"Thanks," I tell him as we pass each other and he pushes up his glasses and nods. His hair follows him on a two-second delay.

I bring my poster to the front of the room and take extra time to set it up—partly because I have to make sure to keep the string around my finger invisible and partly because I'm still thinking about what Peter said. Thankfully, happy tears are the easiest to stop.

Then I take Peter's advice and decide to just have a good time with my presentation.

"Thanks for that, Peter," I start. "If you didn't already guess, he was talking about me. I was his peer reviewer. And he's right— if you show up and keep trying, you can change a lot of things. I know that because I have to try more than the average kid.

"He called me really brave and that's true too." I shrug, like I'm all relaxed. "I mean, not many people could lose a fight as bad as I did and still face coming back to school. Have you *seen* my face? And you know how they say, 'Wait until you see the other guy.' In this case, I *am* the other guy. I don't think *my* other guy even got a hangnail."

A couple of people laugh.

I point to my poster, ignoring my sweaty palms, dry mouth, and the feeling that I really have to pee.

"I studied 'How to be Funny,'" I say, "but I think a lot of you already heard my report the other day in the cafeteria."

"Too bad you aren't funny," Justin shouts out.

Ms. Harding says his name, but I just shrug again like it doesn't bother me. (It only does a tiny bit.) "I agree, Justin, and it's really too bad. I mean, my mom says I was *born* funny. But then I realized she was just talking about the way I *looked*."

I get more laughs. Even Jenna is smiling. From his seat, Peter gives me a thumbs-up.

"So after extensive, painful research of hilarious TV shows and joke books, I'll share what I've found and hope you have better luck than me."

I point to the trifold with my left hand as I jerk the fishing line in my right hand. The line glued to the top of my poster works perfectly to send my poster airborne. My visual aid crashes down on top of me. I purposely—and exaggeratedly—fall to the ground.

"Ummm," I say, scrambling to get up, using too many movements, "that was awkward—which I've learned makes it funny, too." I pull my shirt down to straighten it and set my poster back on the desk—intentionally upside down. "Okay, um . . . my research indicates . . ." I make an exaggerated glance over my shoulder and say, "Oh no!" I say it like I've just now noticed it's the wrong way. I march in a circle like I'm turning around to fix it and the string on my finger pulls the poster behind me so it's trailing like a kite. Now everybody knows it's a joke. They are cracking up. I am too.

After I make a full circle, Ms. Harding crosses her arms and clears her throat. I asked her to do right before we started our presentations.

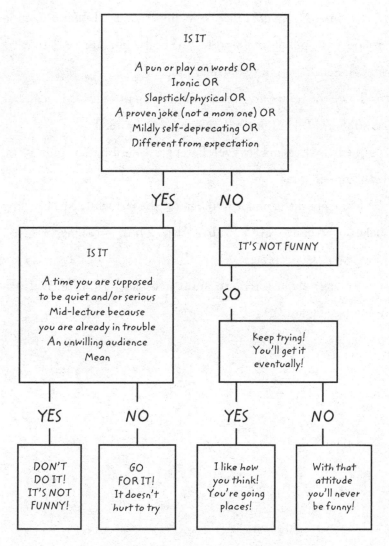

Figure 18. The formula for funny

"Yes. Right," I say, positioning my poster correctly and slipping the fishing line off my finger. "My research shows that self-deprecation and slapstick humor are the most successful. So is appropriate timing." I glance at my teacher. "Like no goofing around in the middle of a report." She nods right on cue. "Knowing your audience is a pretty big deal too. . . ."

I give the rest of my presentation. It's a little less comical, but it's still fun. When I finish, I give an exaggerated bow.

Justin looks as mad as ever. Peter gives me another thumbs-up. Jenna smiles at me.

I take my poster and lean it against the rest while Ms. Harding makes everybody—even Justin—clap. I hear a couple of "good jobs" as I go to my seat.

So, after about a million and three mess-ups, I did it. I was funny (see Figure 18).

ADDITIONAL RESEARCH AND INFORMATION

Include any other important observations and/or notes.

I'M ONE OF the first to the cafeteria. I could sit at the normal table and save room for Peter. But I don't.

I pick another table. One that is usually empty.

Justin is the first to notice me. He smirks like he's won some competition.

"I like it," Peter says sitting down next to me. "A little change. It's brighter over here."

"Definitely less crowded," I say.

I see Jenna before she sees us. She's already put her tray in the normal place and is about to sit next to Fred. Good old Fred is looking relaxed as ever—just like he did during his presentation about paper towel absorbencies, and during the lecture following his presentation where Ms. Harding said we should push ourselves a little if we ever want to make a difference in the world. I couldn't tell if he didn't know the speech was for him or if he did and he just didn't care.

Jenna catches my eyes. She hesitates but then picks up her tray. When she sits on the other side of Peter she says, "Sometimes you are funny. But usually it's when you don't mean to be."

I laugh. "Thank you for your honesty."

She smiles too. "Any time."

"Oh, I've been meaning to ask you something," Peter says. "Did you really write notes about all of us in your notebook?"

I really want to lie. I might have before, but I want to be better than that now. Me, But Better . . . but in the best possible way. "Yes."

"Cool," Peter bites off the hummus end of a carrot. "Can I read it?"

If this same conversation happened a day later, I'd be able to say I didn't have it, but with my still-broken locker and today's presentation, I have it with me. I slide it across the table to him. Jenna leans over to look too. Well, it was fun to have friends while it lasted.

They read the Exit-lence notes first. Peter laughs; Jenna scowls. Then they flip the pages, scanning through all of my notes. When they get to the page about them, my palms sweat. I'm quiet as they read.

When they're done, Peter nods, flips through a couple more pages, and slides the notebook back to me.

"That was before I knew you."

"Okay."

"So are you mad at me?"

He looks at me like I'm crazy. "What would I be mad at you? You wrote about why I was funny."

"Yeah, but . . ." I don't want to say the rest because maybe he didn't see that part. But this is where it matters. It's not one big change, it's every little decision that makes me better. I grimace and force myself to keep going. "I said people were laughing at you."

"So."

"That doesn't bother you?"

He shrugs. "Why would it? I made people laugh."

Relief floods me all the way down to my fingers. It makes me brave enough to ask Jenna if we are still good.

She shrugs. "Yup. Nothing you said is untrue."

I wouldn't believe her, but it's Jenna. I know I can trust her.

"By the way," she says stabbing the straw into her milk carton. "My dad keeps asking if I've seen your mom again. I don't really like it."

I'm not sure how to respond to that. "Okay."

Some kids I don't know sit in the empty chairs. We all say hi but I mainly talk to Peter and Jenna.

When the lunch bell rings, we all get up and shuffle to the cafeteria doors.

"Your presentation was great," somebody behind me says. I turn around to say thank you. It's Justin. Before I speak, he adds, "For me. Not you. For you it was embarrassing." He laughs at his own joke as he walks past me. Riley follows him. She rolls her eyes but doesn't say anything at all.

I pause to wait for Jenna and Peter catch up so we can walk back to class together.

We make our way through the same hall I walked into on the first day. The same hall that felt too tight and too scary. It's different walking down it with friends though. Here we are: the boy that's not funny, the boy that's a weirdo, and the girl obsessed with the truth. It totally seems like this would never work, but the results show that it does.

IMPORTANT EQUATIONS

Me - Moving = Crisis
Mom + Lip Naw = Stressed/Sad
Fred x Anything = Cool
Jenna + Truth = Obsessed
Peter + Video Games = Happy
Me + Peter = Fun
Me x Grit = Greatness

Figure 19. Current data

Who knows? Further research may even show that Justin and Fred and Riley belong with us too. Then again, maybe not. More data is definitely needed before we reach that conclusion (see Figure 19). Luckily, since Mom and I are staying, we have lots of time to figure it out.

From: herecomeztreble@nma.com
To: nomadman@nma.com
Subject: Reality

> Do you remember whenever Mr. Bob messed up and he'd make fun of himself and say, "Those who can't, teach?" Turns out that was true.

> Truth bomb: Moving was really hard. It still is. It took me forever to fit in, and I still don't know if I do.

> I couldn't tell you that when you first got to Fort Worth. If I had, you'd know that I had sort of exaggerated (aka lied) since I moved. I promise I didn't mean to hide the truth. I think I was embarrassed or something. Like you wouldn't like me as much if you knew.

I'm sorry it took so long to e-mail back. It took a while for me to be brave enough to tell you.

And I still definitely want you to come down. But I totally get if you don't want to see ME.

(Not Mr. T) Just Trent

— — — — — — — — — — — — —

From: nomadman@nma.com
To: herecomeztreble@nma.com
Subject: Re: Reality

Mr. T—

Thank you.

Actually, BEFORE I say thank you, let me be honest.

I've been freaked out that you weren't going to e-mail me back. Then when you did and I read what you wrote, I sort of hated you for about seventeen seconds. I wanted to call off the summer visit and delete your e-mail address from the computer memory.

But I get it—why you told me everything was so great even when it wasn't.

I feel like if you had told me the truth, I could have helped you. Or you would have helped me.

But maybe that's not true.

Maybe I wouldn't have understood until I went through it too.

Normal life is hard. It's boring. It's day after day of nothing special. No finish lines or moving dates. No being the exciting new guy.

So I guess, thank you for letting me figure that out myself. And for telling me the truth now.

The weird thing is that now that I know that life is boring AND that I'm not all that great, I'm not as afraid of failing in it. Mainly because I know I WILL. Because that's just who I am.

BUT the thing about who I am is I don't have to stay the same. I can be better. Not in a grand gesture or a complete change sort of way. It is a day to day, moment to moment thing. It's a decision to make a better decision next time.

Does June 8th work for me to come down? Mom is going to book my ticket tonight.

Ross

ACKNOWLEDGMENTS

There are several people I want to thank, because This Book – You = Not Exist.

To those who made this my book, but better. My agent, Emily Keyes. There was an attempt—and you made it into a reality. I am so grateful to work with you. My editor, Alyson Heller. You helped make this book into the something I hoped it could be. Regina Flath, the artist who created the cover. It is beautiful. And to all those at Simon & Schuster. Thank you for investing your time, energy, and skills.

To my fellow writers. Suzanne Frank, my mentor and friend. Your words have always been a gift. Jenny Bellamy, you are a force . . . in the best way. You were the first to get me to admit my little secret/double life: I am a writer. Your quote is still in my office for whenever I doubt that. Magnificent 11 members, I'm so glad to be on this journey with you. Without you, Amy Anderson, I might not have boarded that plane to New York. Keith Goodnight, Kay Honeyman, Amanda Arista, and Amanda Alvarez— my first critique group. I don't know how I got to join such amazing writers when I was so new. You taught me how to listen and think like an author.

To the people who encourage me daily. Brooke Fossey, my beta reader, my office mate, my reality check, and my best friend. Sometimes I scare myself by imagining what it would be like if I hadn't met you. Thank God (literally) that I did. Kim Henke, Shelly Levy, Robyn Scott, and Kate Wallace. My community. This book wouldn't exist without your prayers, love, and support. Melissa and Duane Pekar, you have celebrated with me, brainstormed with me, and taught me to pause to and be thankful. And to those that have cheered me on—Chelsea, Brandon, Emily, Travis, Ben, Michael, Sean, Dustin, and Kristie.

To those who have been there from the beginning. My earliest beta readers: Krista Guass, Tim Watson, and Nathan Monroe. I'm sorry I made you read that stuff. Somehow, you always thought of nice things to say. And Mr. Monroe, you influenced me as a writer and as a person. Thank you for everything you taught me in that "peculiar language."

To all my family. To Sheryl for your example as a fantastic mom(ma) and a hardworking, strong woman. You've always believed in me. And Bill, you became my family during my most awkward years. I finally keep my room clean. Sort of. Lee, my dad, you gave me both your walk and wit. And Lynne, you love and care for us fiercely. My sister, Angela, thank you for laughing at my jokes even when they weren't funny (giraffe). And Kevin for being a steady presence and always having our back. And to Mimi. You gave me the artist-type gene. I hope one day to write as beautifully as you paint. I could fill pages with all you have done for me. My grandfathers, Poppa and Popeye, who were both as wonderful as Pops. I miss you both. And to some of my favorite kiddos—Hannah, Aubree, Brady, Rhett, and Eva. You provide lots of joy, fun, and ideas. Fred and Vicki, for letting a writer-type into your family despite the crazy I bring. Grandlee, for your unending excitement. Bri, the greatest SIL/former roommate. And Nick, who, when I said I wanted to be an author but probably couldn't, asked, "Why not?"

To the Camp Allbright crew. In my mind we are all still kids painting cups, skiddidling, and swapping secrets. Peg used to make me keep the Camp Allbright journal. Maybe she knew I'd be a writer before I did. I know she's proud we are sticking together.

And to the four that I am truly blessed to do life with each day. My husband, Zach. I may have a way cooler job than you—but I couldn't do mine if you didn't do yours. And to my children, Colton, Logan, and Rowyn. I am so very happy to be your mom. I'm endlessly grateful for your joy, your love, and your existence.